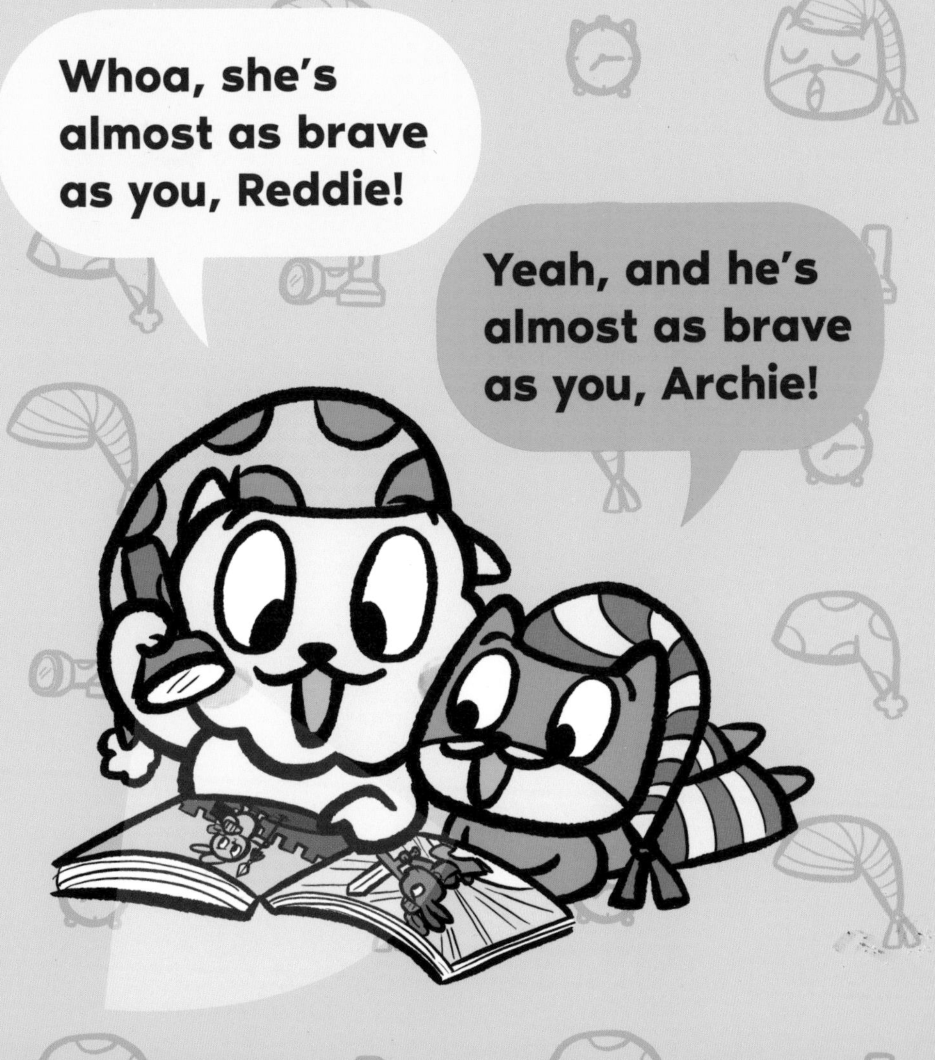
Whoa, she's almost as brave as you, Reddie!
Yeah, and he's almost as brave as you, Archie!

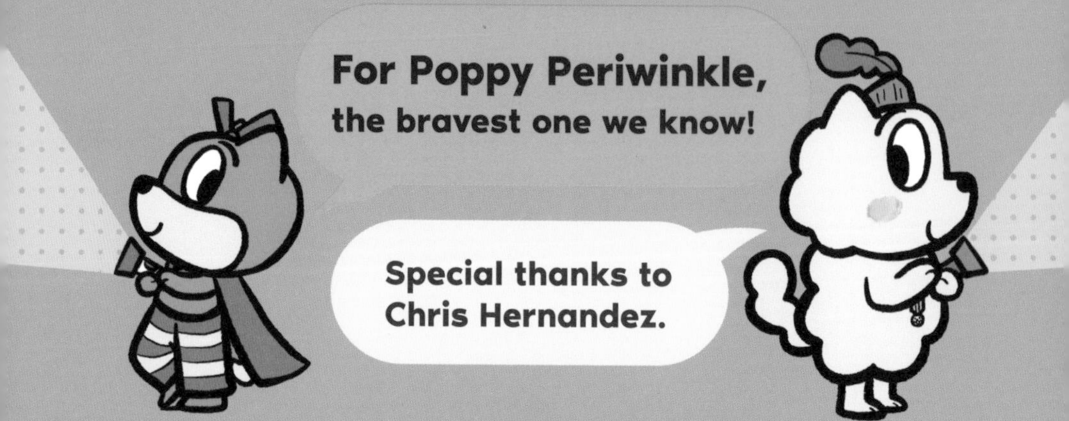

For Poppy Periwinkle,
the bravest one we know!

Special thanks to
Chris Hernandez.

RAZORBILL

An imprint of Penguin Random House LLC, New York

First published in the United States of America by Razorbill, an imprint of Penguin Random House LLC, 2022

Copyright © 2022 by Candy Robertson and Nicholas James Robertson

Visit us online at penguinrandomhouse.com.

Library of Congress Cataloging-in-Publication Data
Names: Robertson, Nicholas James, author, illustrator.
Title: It doesn't scare me! : a discovery! / pictures and words by Candy James. Other titles: It does not scare me!
Description: New York : Razorbill, 2022. | Series: Archie & Reddie ; book 4 | Audience: Ages 4-8 years |
Summary: When Archie is woken by a scary noise in the night, he turns
to his fox friend Reddie to help him get to the bottom of it.
Identifiers: LCCN 2021046692 | ISBN 9780593350201 (hardcover) |
ISBN 9780593350225 (ebook) | ISBN 9780593350218 (ebook)
Subjects: CYAC: Graphic novels. | Foxes–Fiction. | Fear–Fiction. | Friendship–Fiction. | Humorous stories. |
Mystery and detective stories. | LCGFT: Funny animal comics. | Graphic novels.
Classification: LCC PZ7.7.R6325 It 2022 | DDC 741.5/994–dc23/eng/20211006
LC record available at https://lccn.loc.gov/2021046692

Manufactured in China

1 3 5 7 9 10 8 6 4 2

TOPL

Book design by Candy James. Text set in Noir Pro.

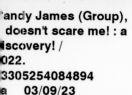
ARCHIE **& REDDIE** BOOK

IT DOESN'T
SCARE ME!

A DISCOVERY!

PICTURES AND WORDS BY
CANDY JAMES

RAZORBILL

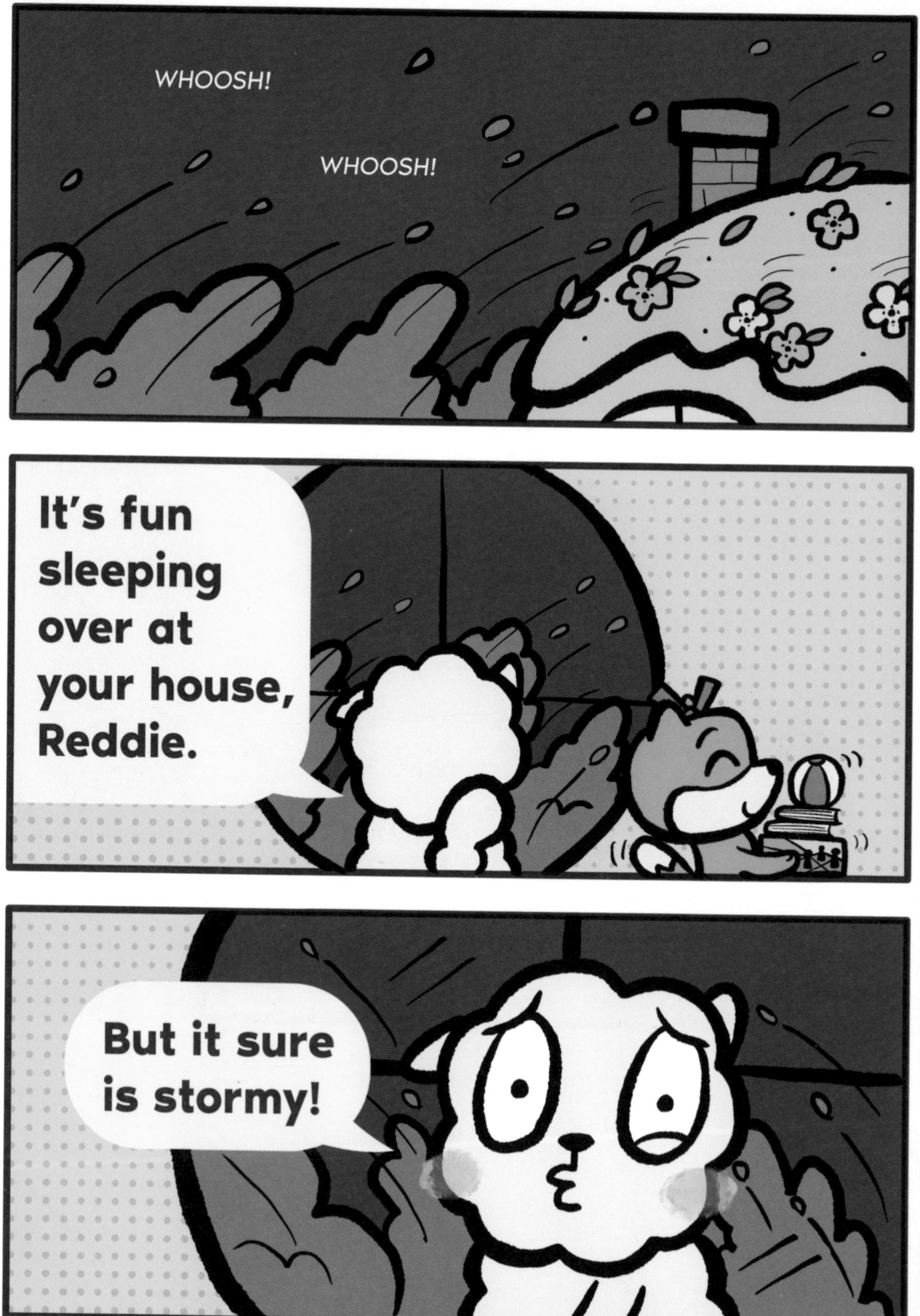
WHOOSH!
WHOOSH!
It's fun sleeping over at your house, Reddie.
But it sure is stormy!

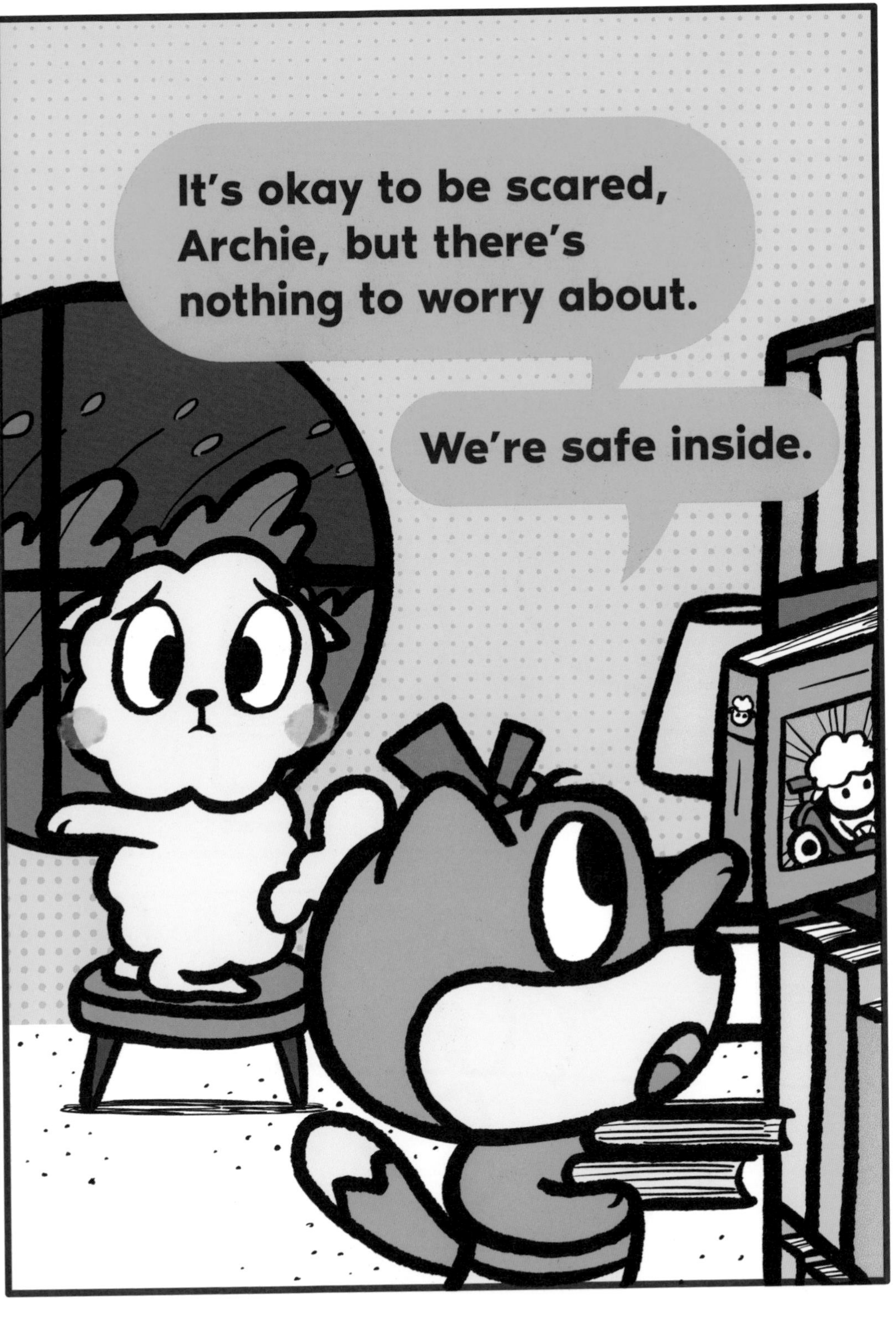
It's okay to be scared, Archie, but there's nothing to worry about.
We're safe inside.

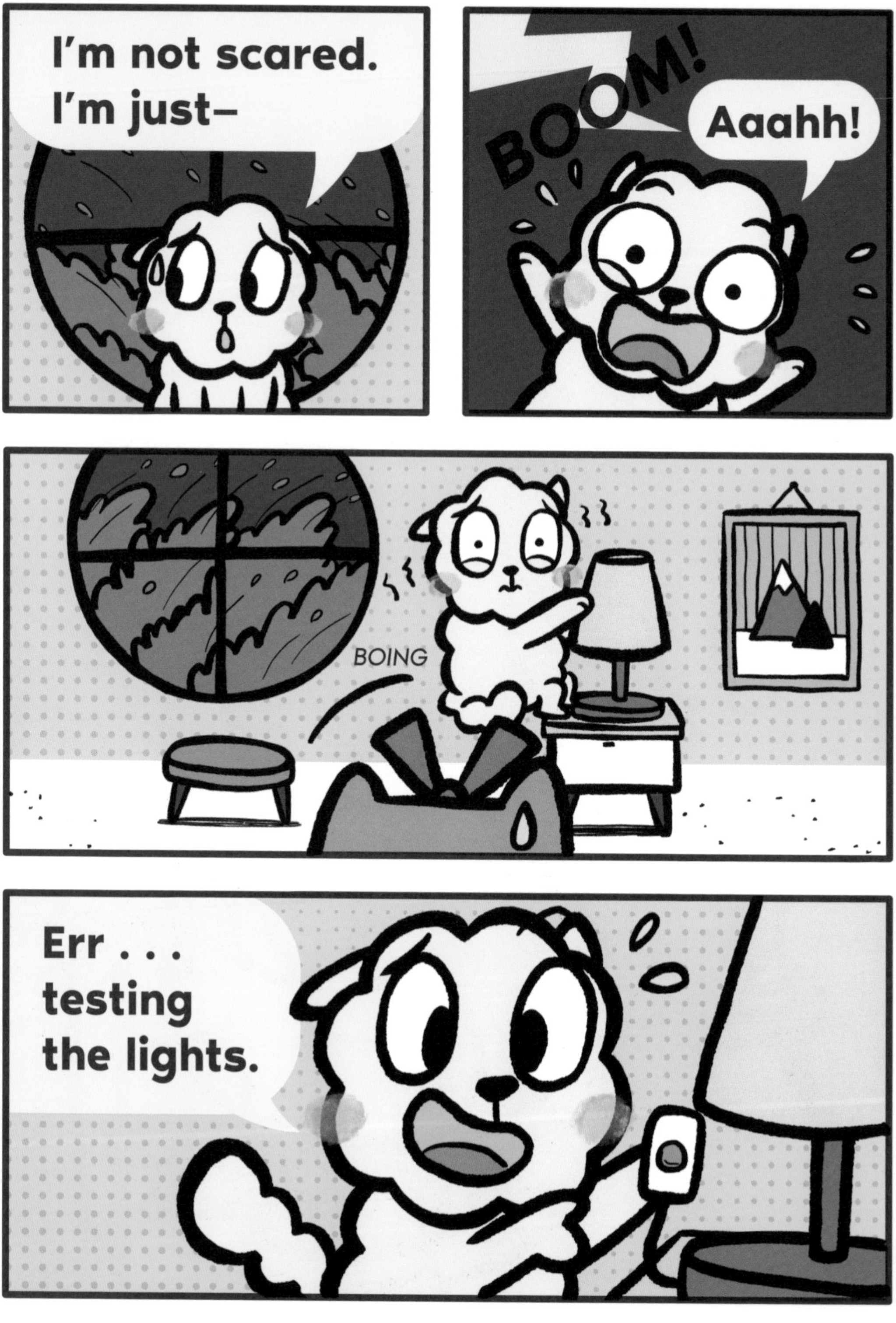

I'm not scared. I'm just–
BOOM!
Aaahh!
BOING
Err . . . testing the lights.

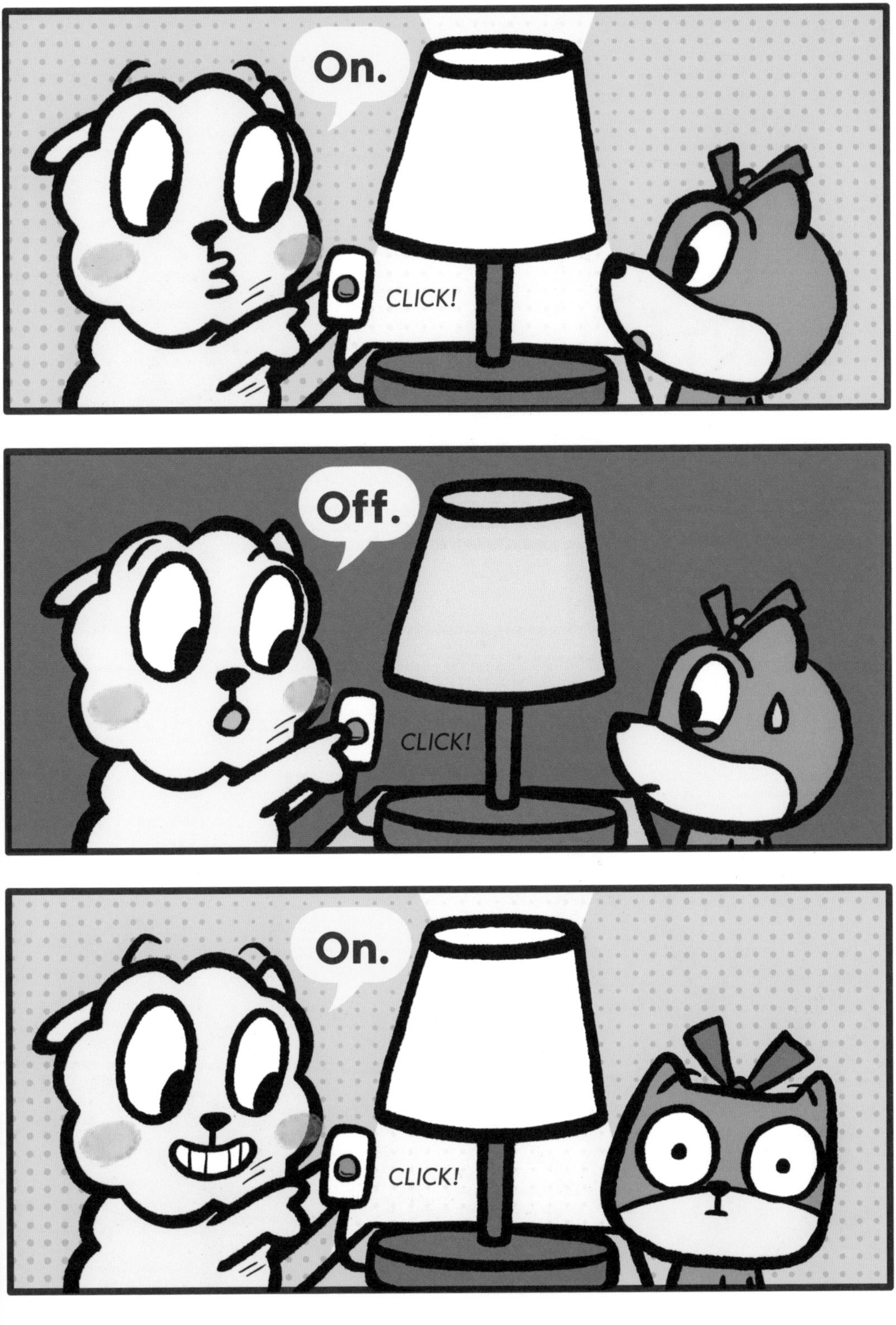
On.
CLICK!
Off.
CLICK!
On.
CLICK!

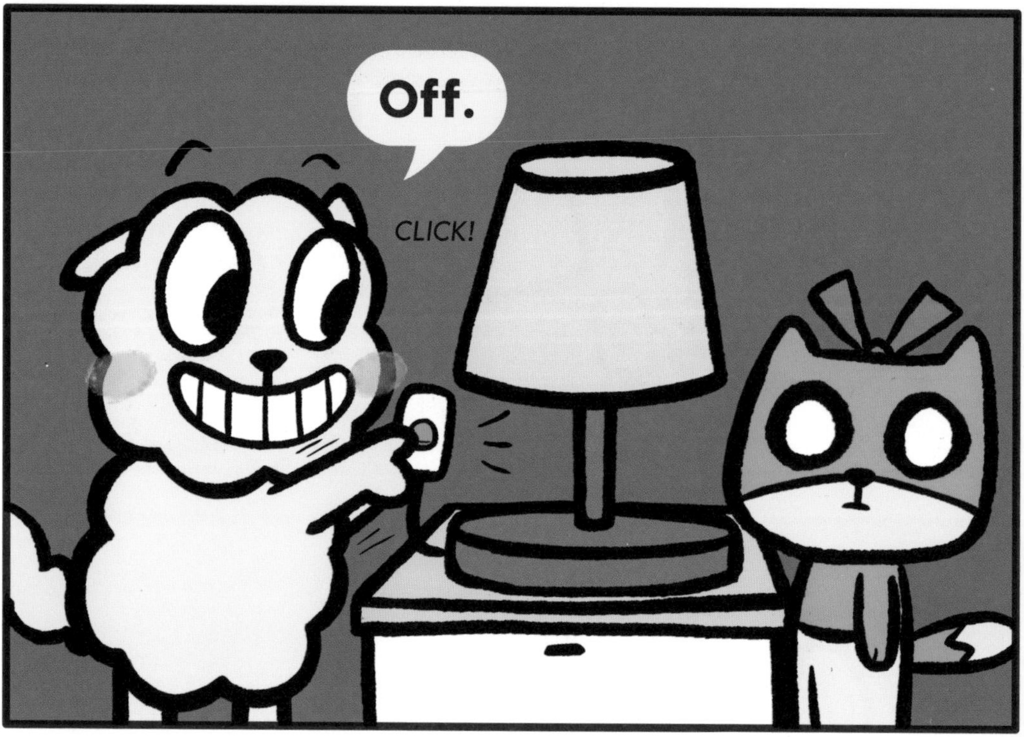
Off.
CLICK!

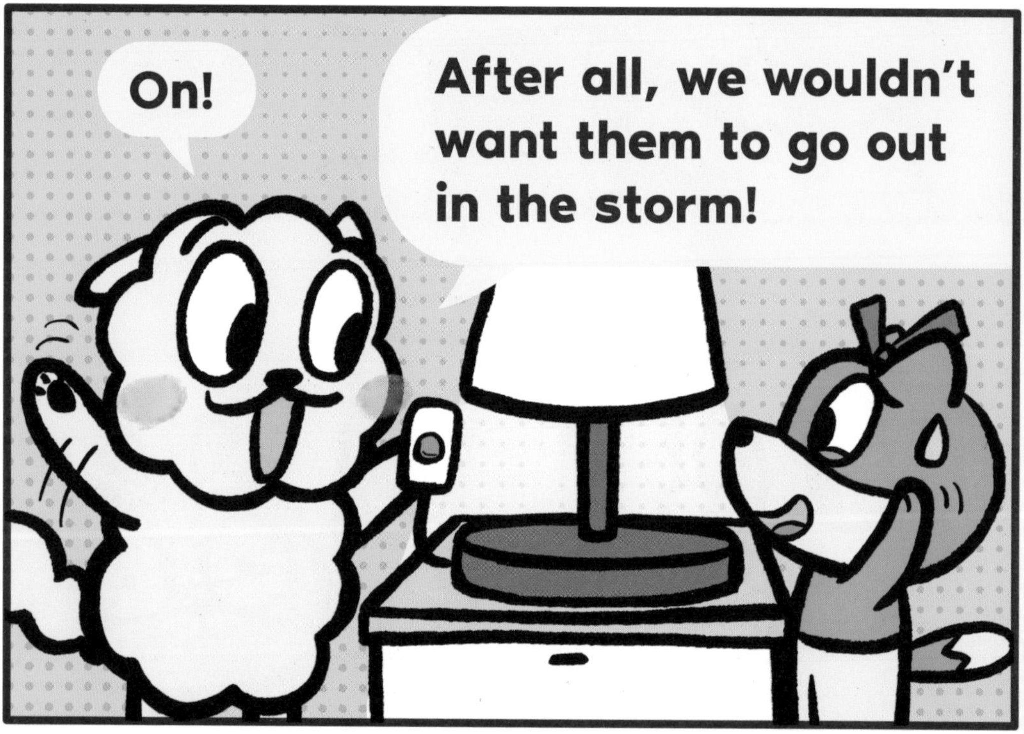
On!
After all, we wouldn't want them to go out in the storm!

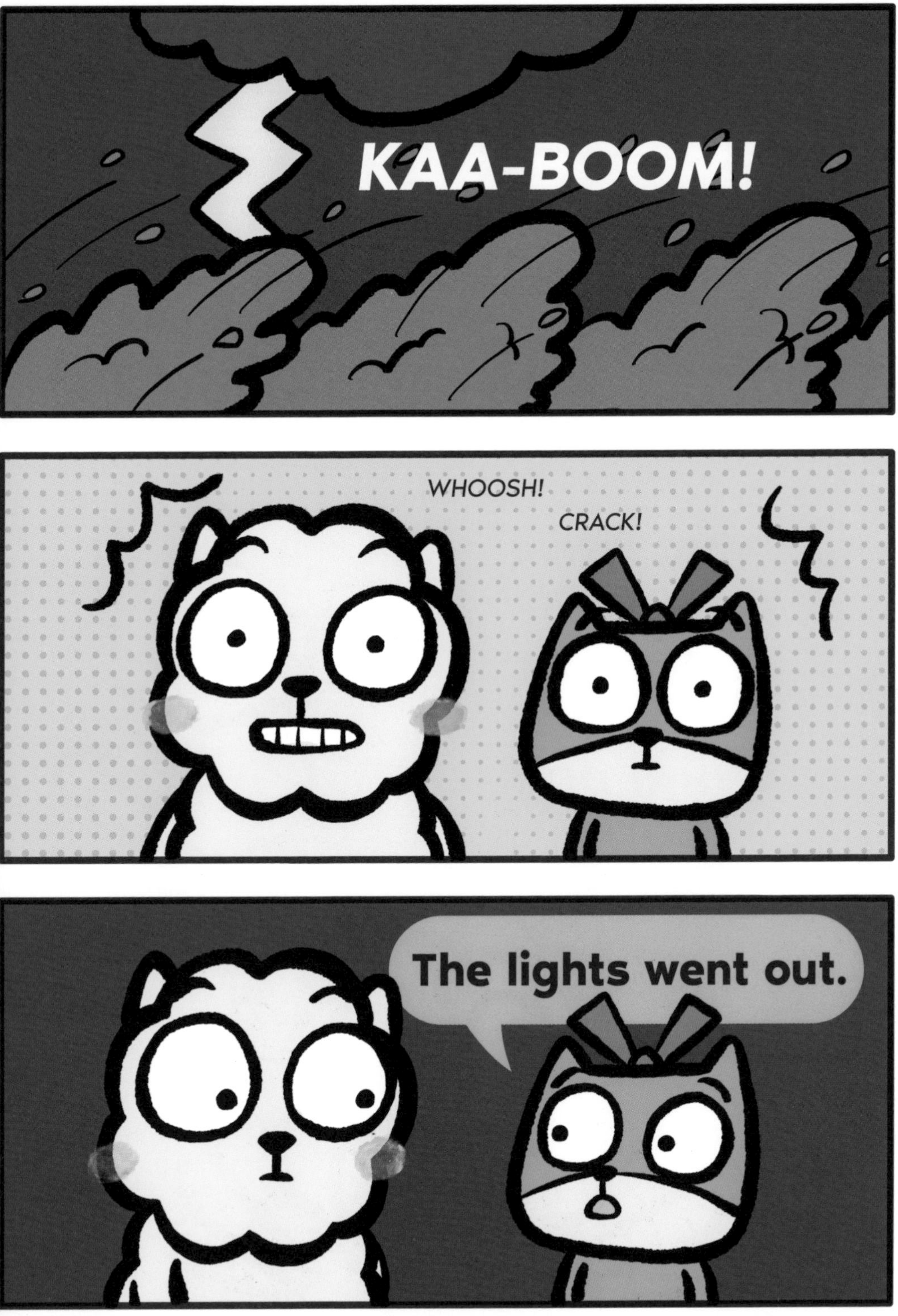
KAA-BOOM!
WHOOSH!
CRACK!
The lights went out.

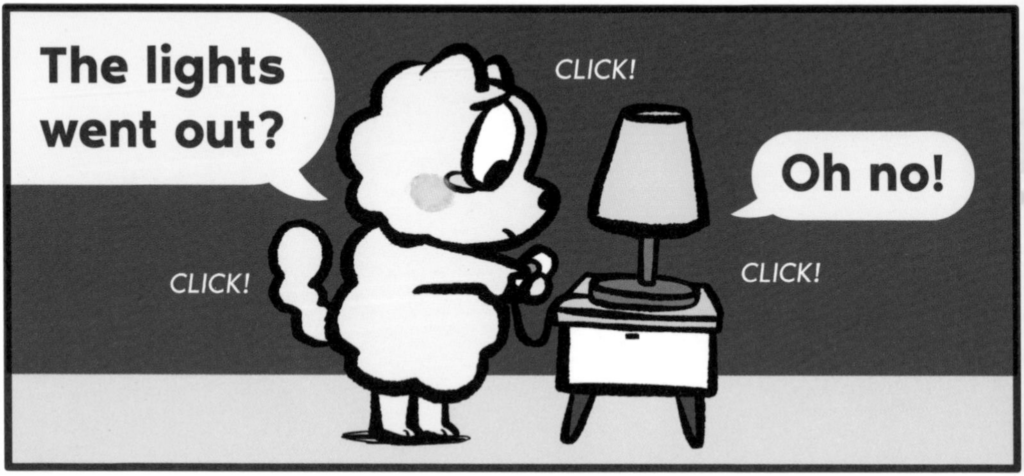
The lights went out?
CLICK!
CLICK!
Oh no!
CLICK!

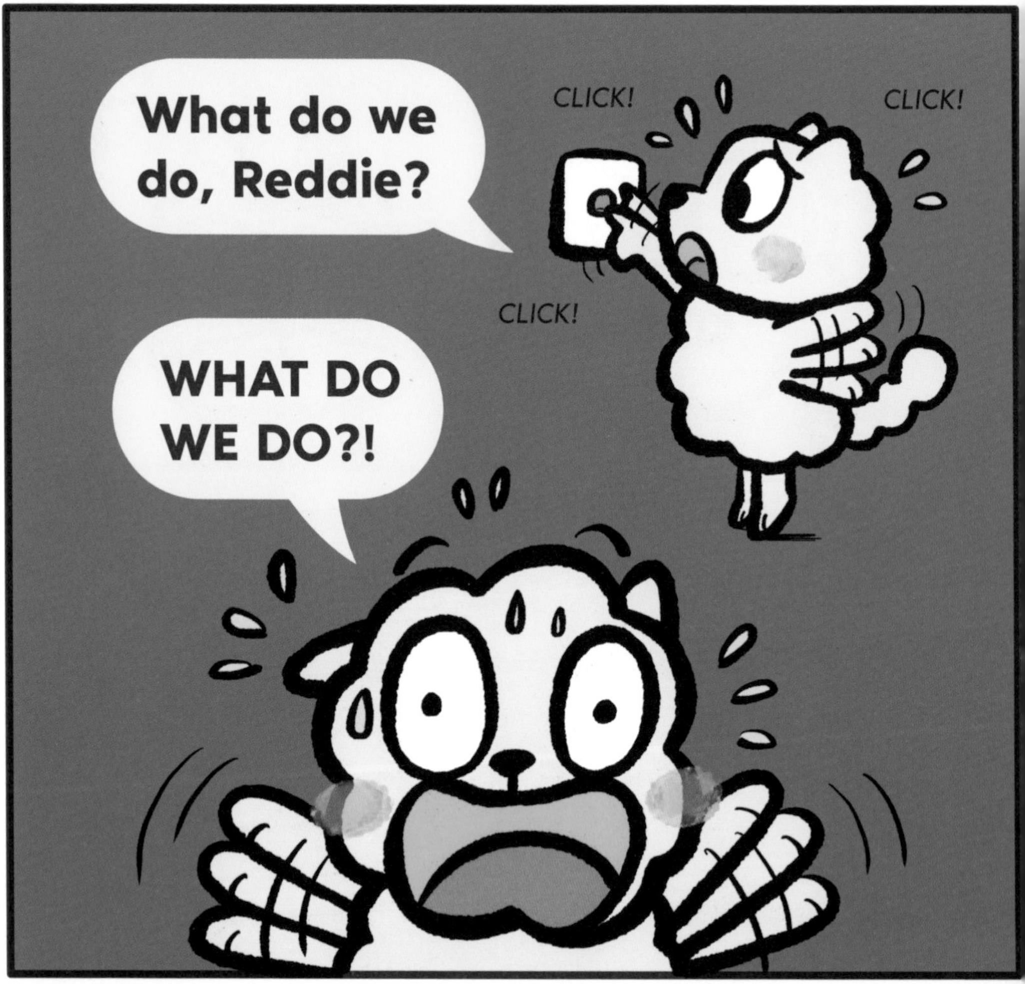
What do we do, Reddie?
CLICK!
CLICK!
CLICK!
WHAT DO WE DO?!

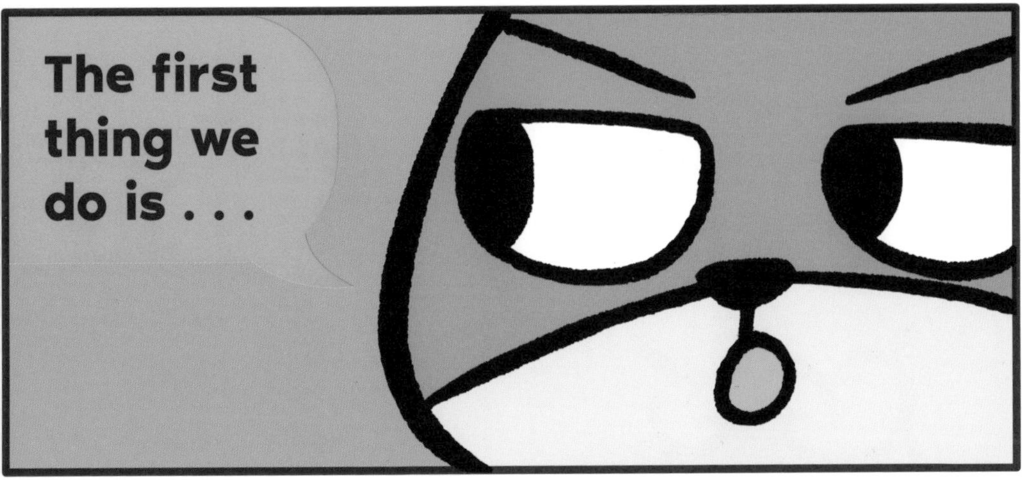
The first thing we do is . . .

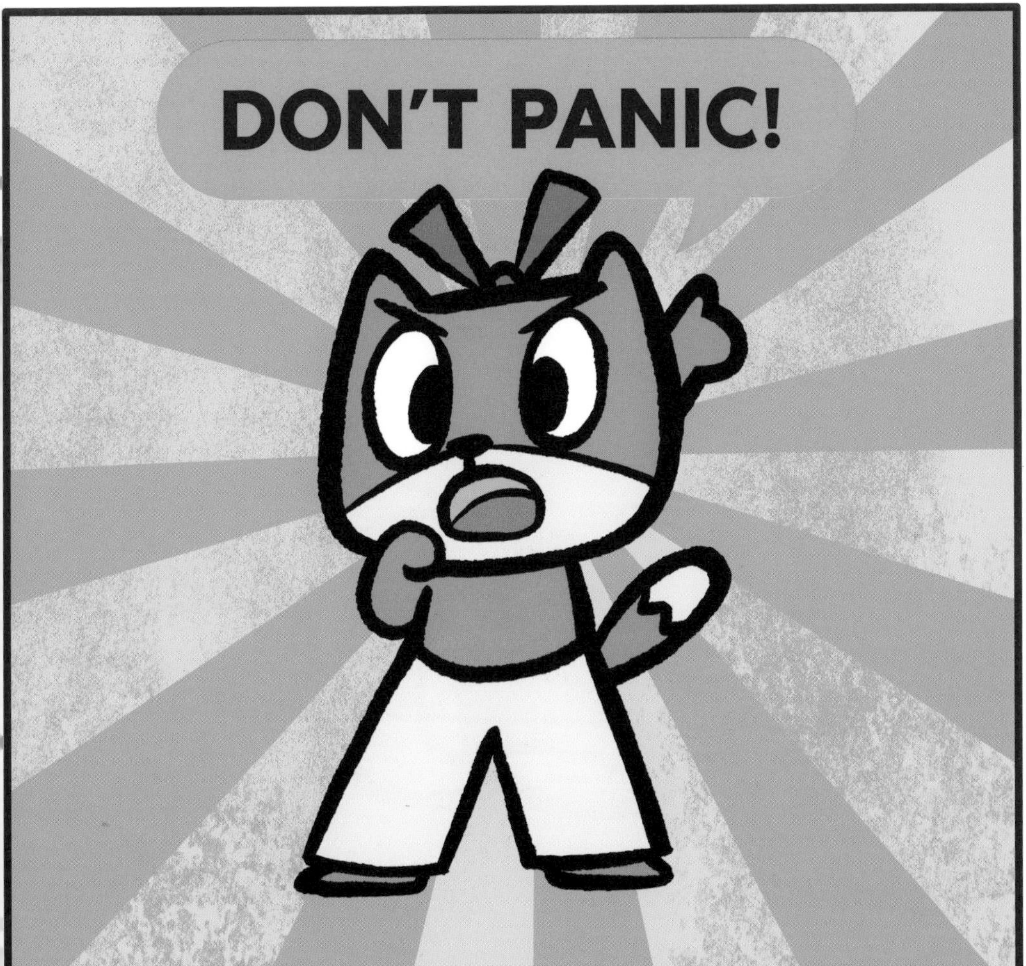
DON'T PANIC!

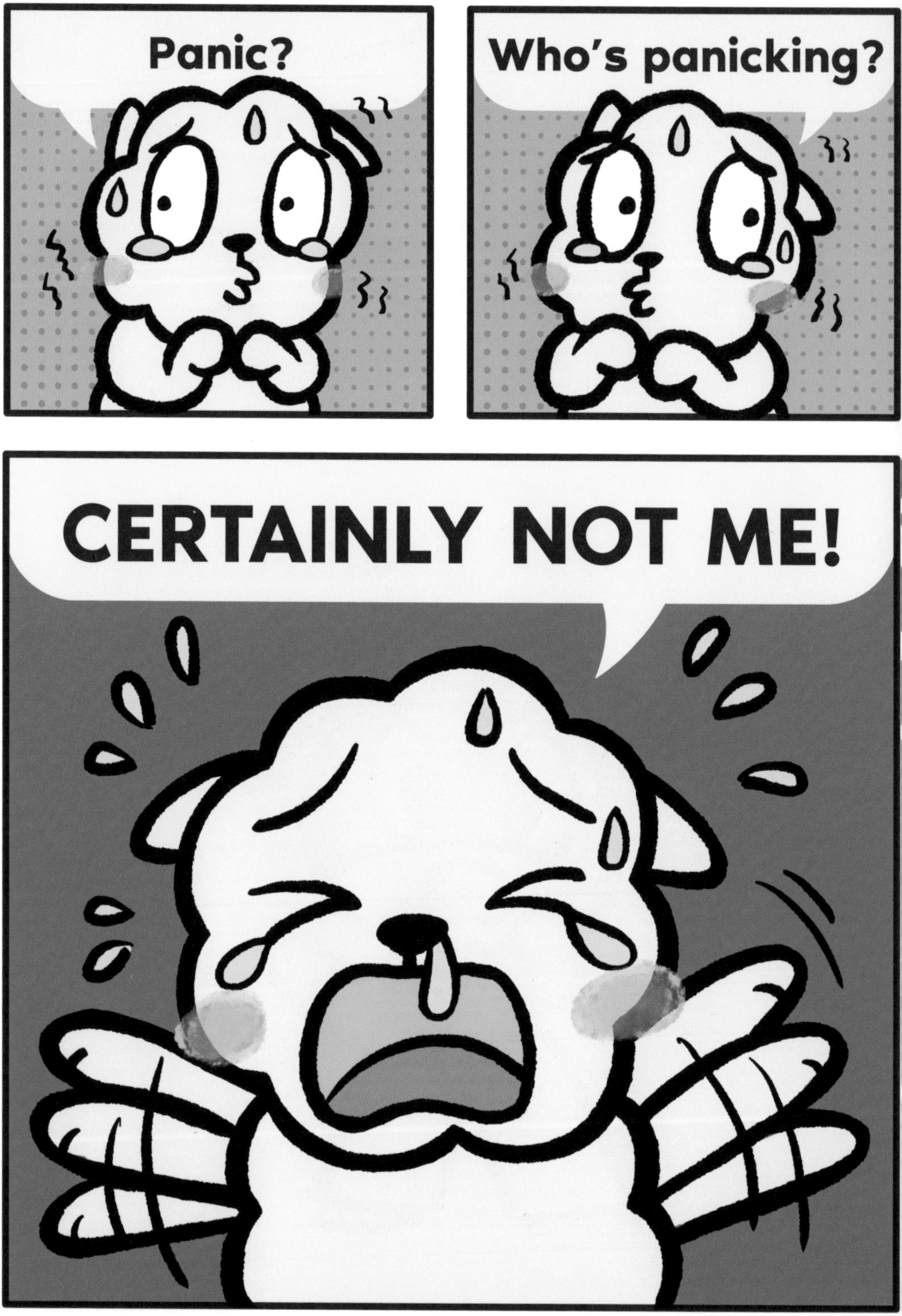
Panic?
Who's panicking?
CERTAINLY NOT ME!

That's good.

But if you do,

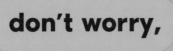

don't worry,

because we have . . .

CLICK!

CLICK!

THESE!

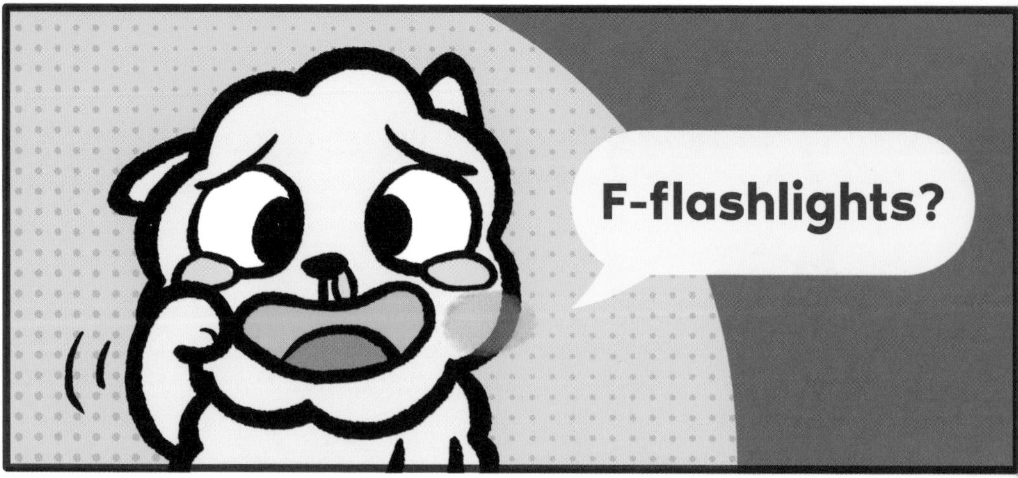
F-flashlights?

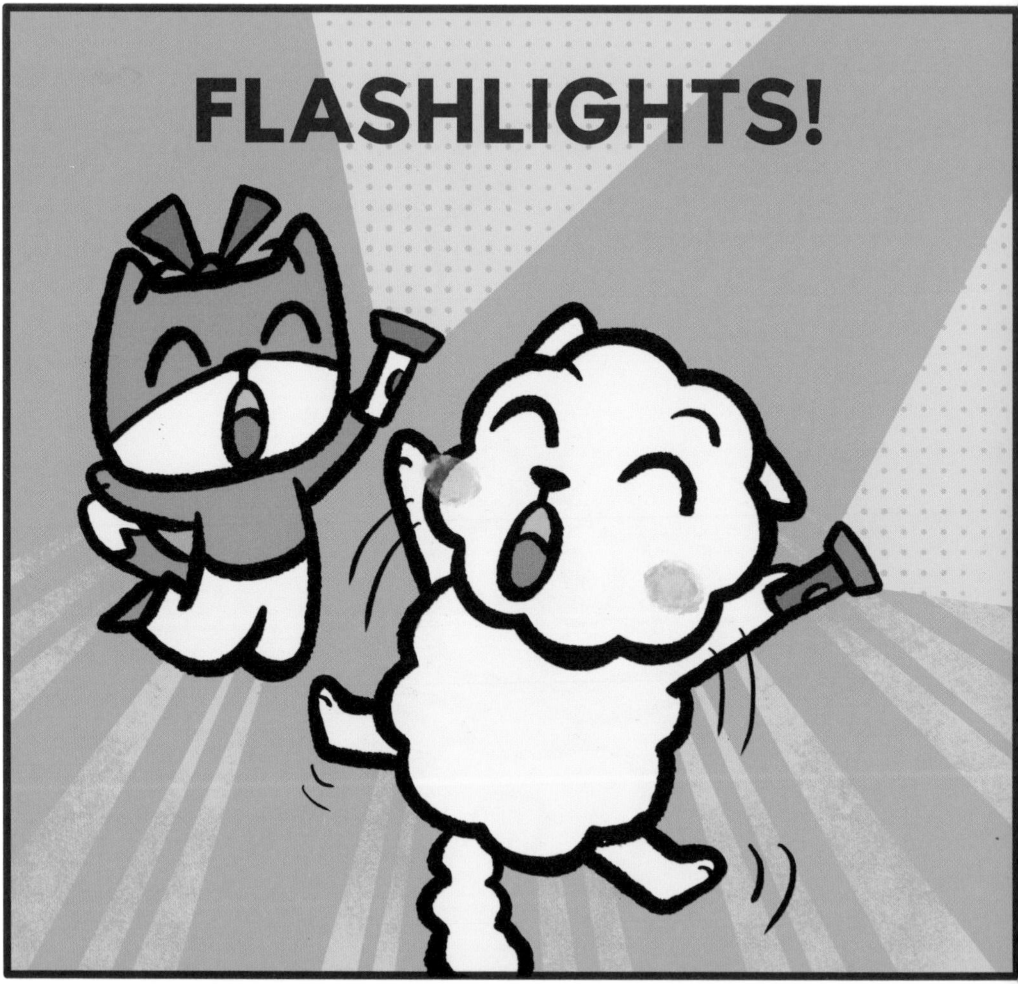
FLASHLIGHTS!

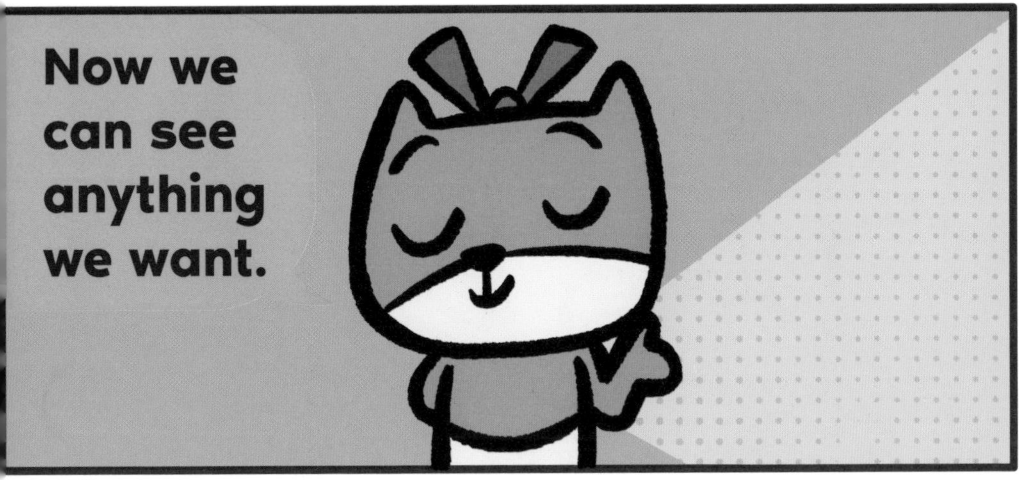
Now we can see anything we want.

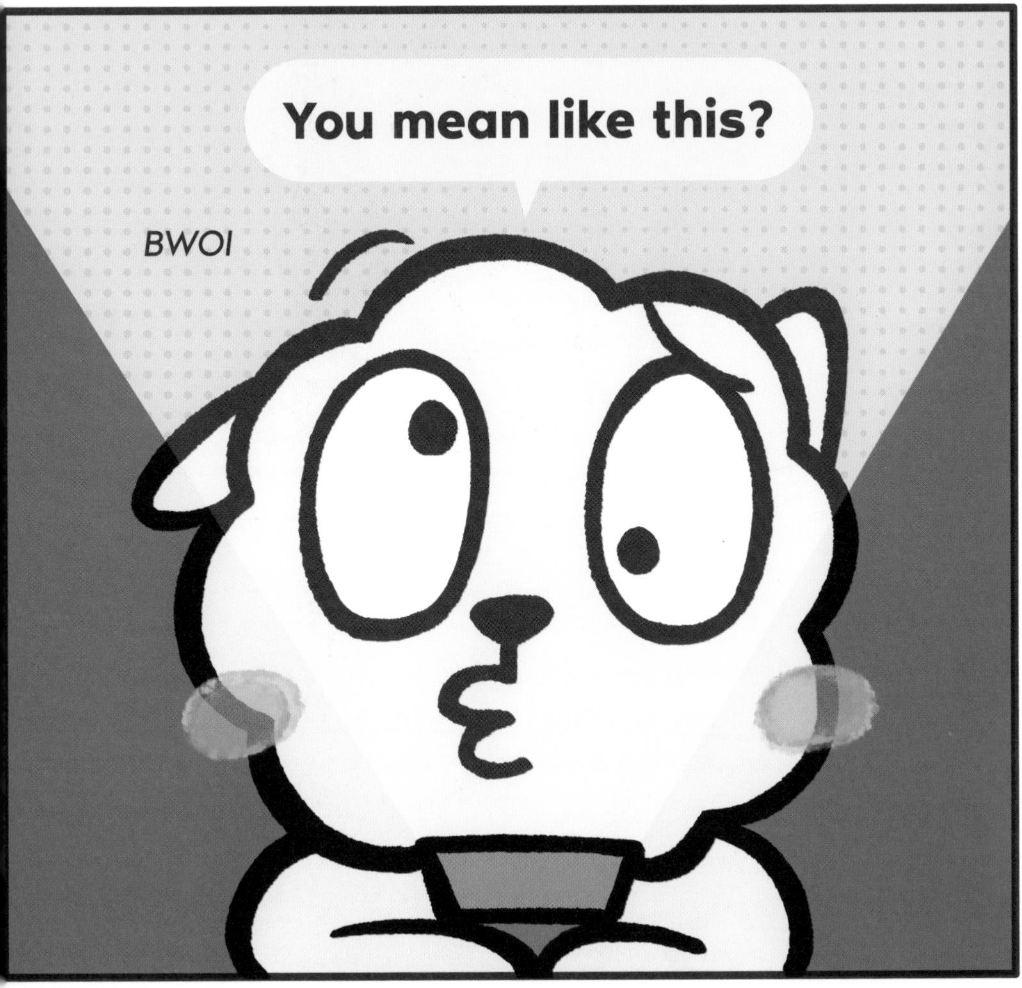
You mean like this?
BWOI

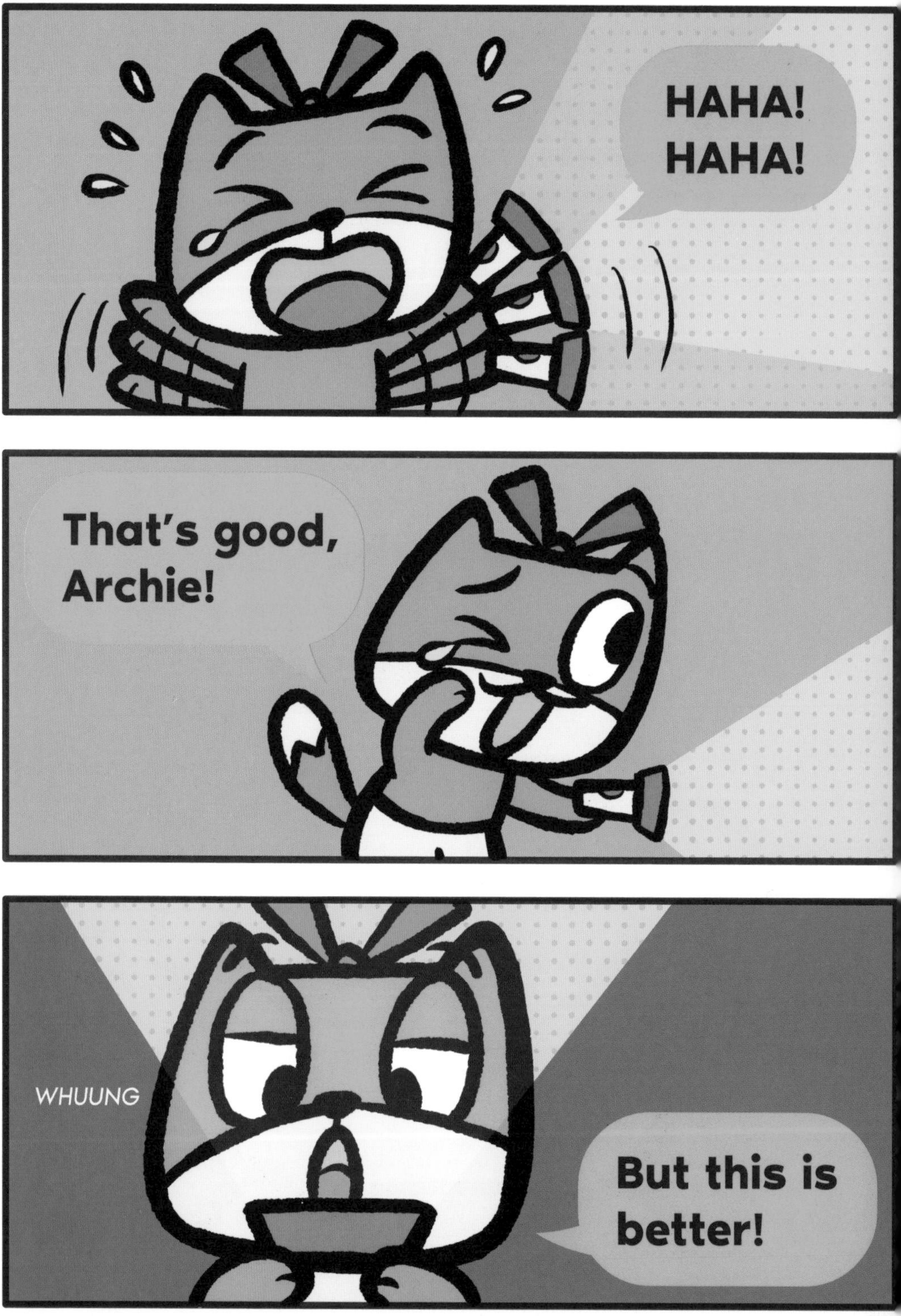
HAHA! HAHA!
That's good, Archie!
WHUUNG
But this is better!

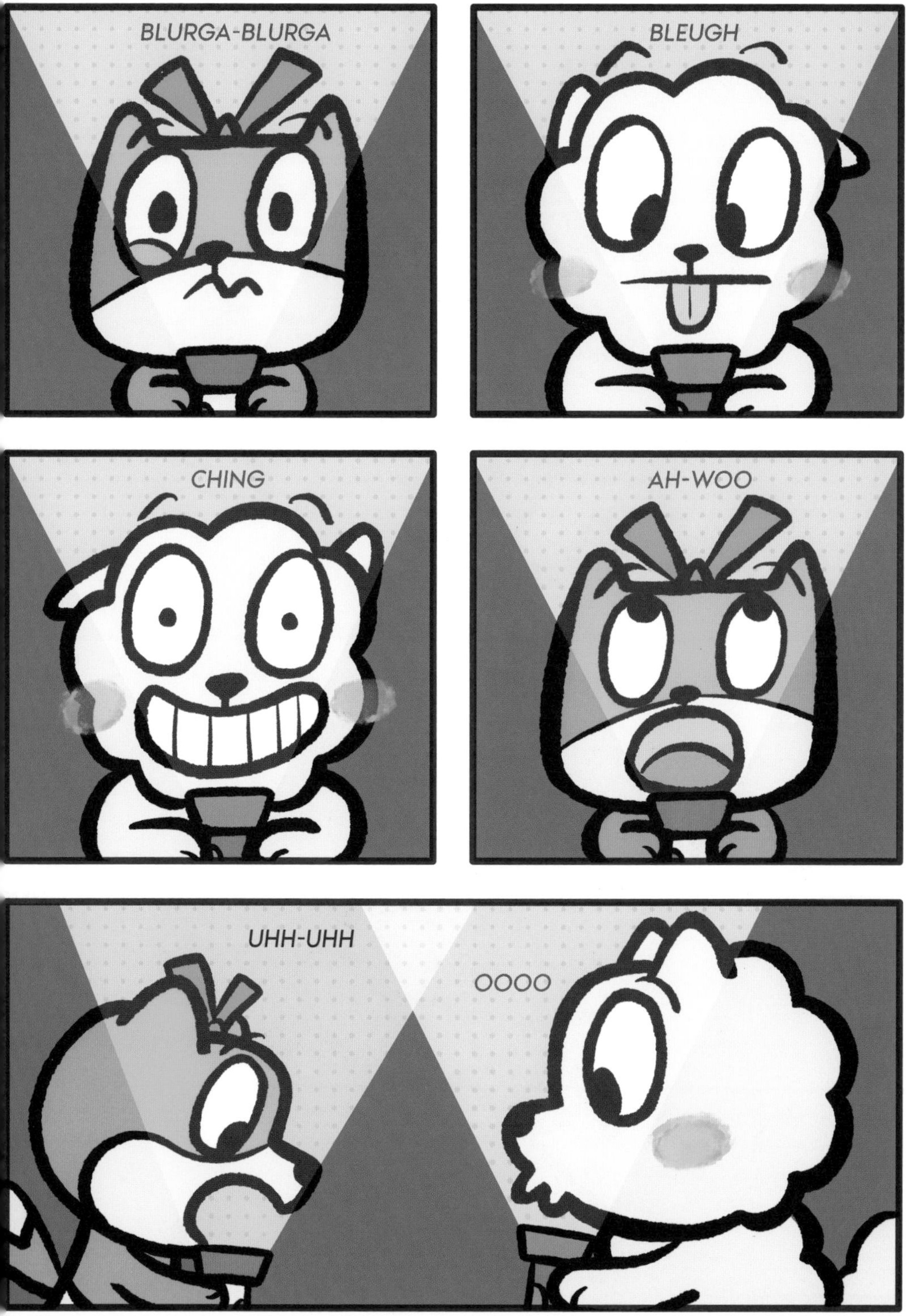
BLURGA-BLURGA
BLEUGH
CHING
AH-WOO
UHH-UHH
OOOO

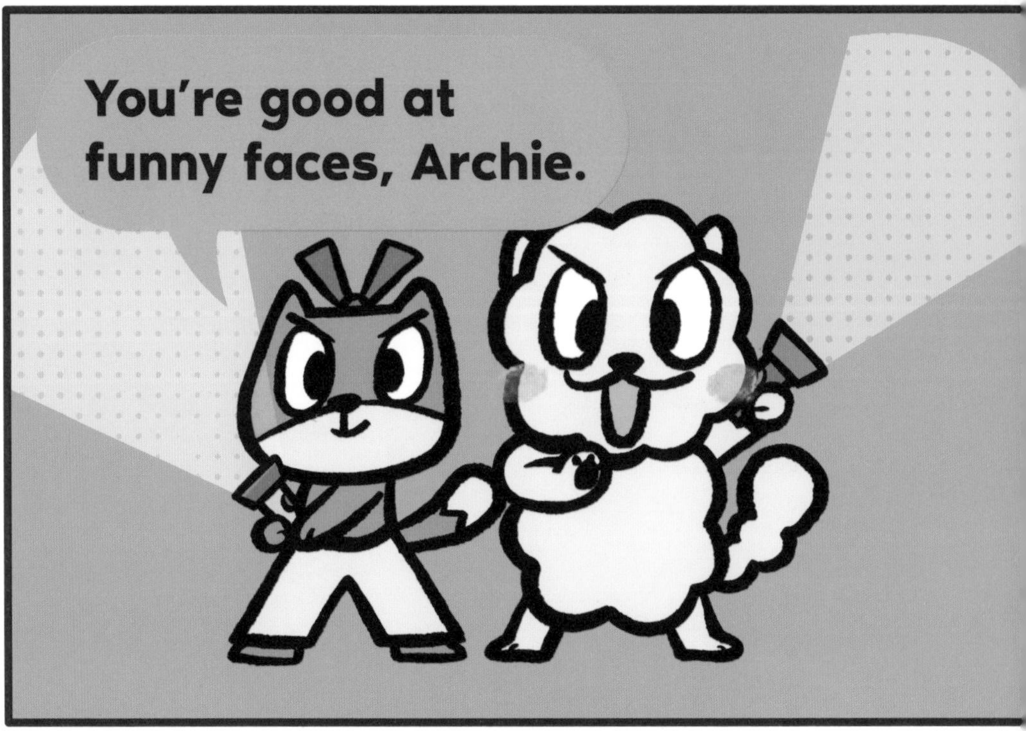
You're good at funny faces, Archie.

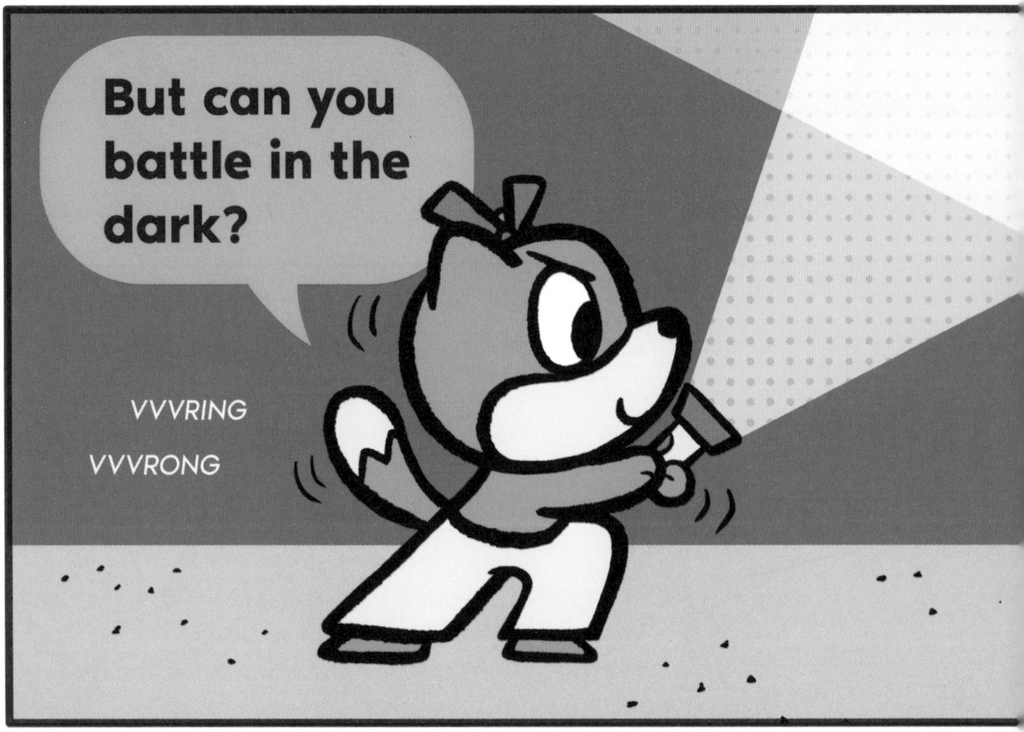
But can you battle in the dark?
VVVRING
VVVRONG

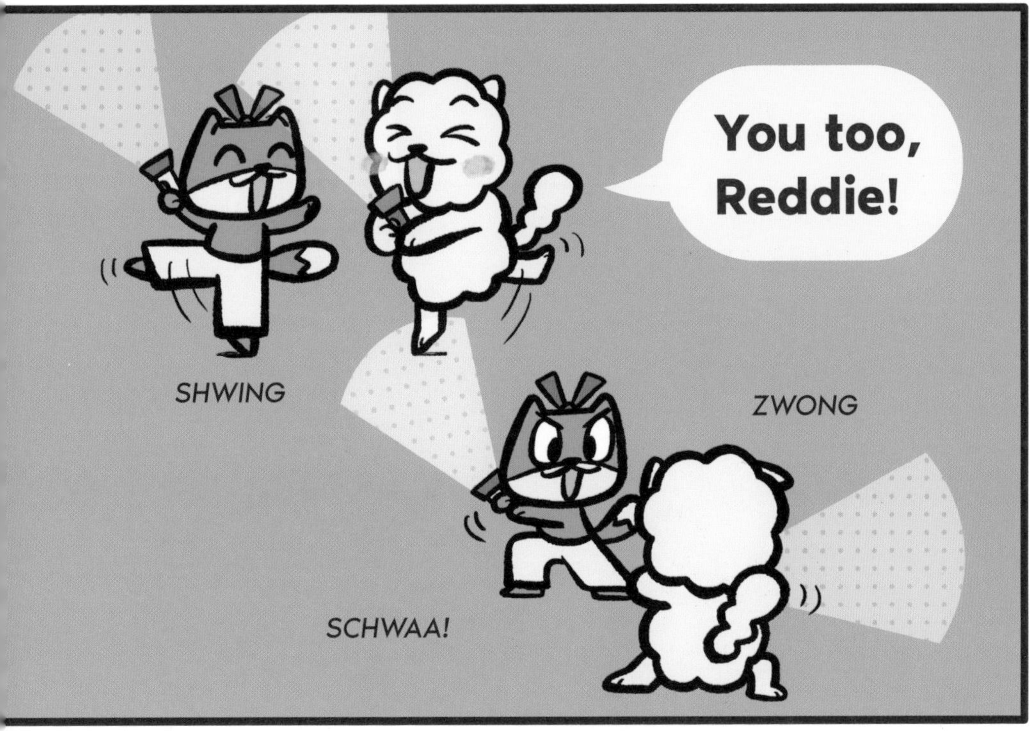
You too, Reddie!
SHWING
ZWONG
SCHWAA!

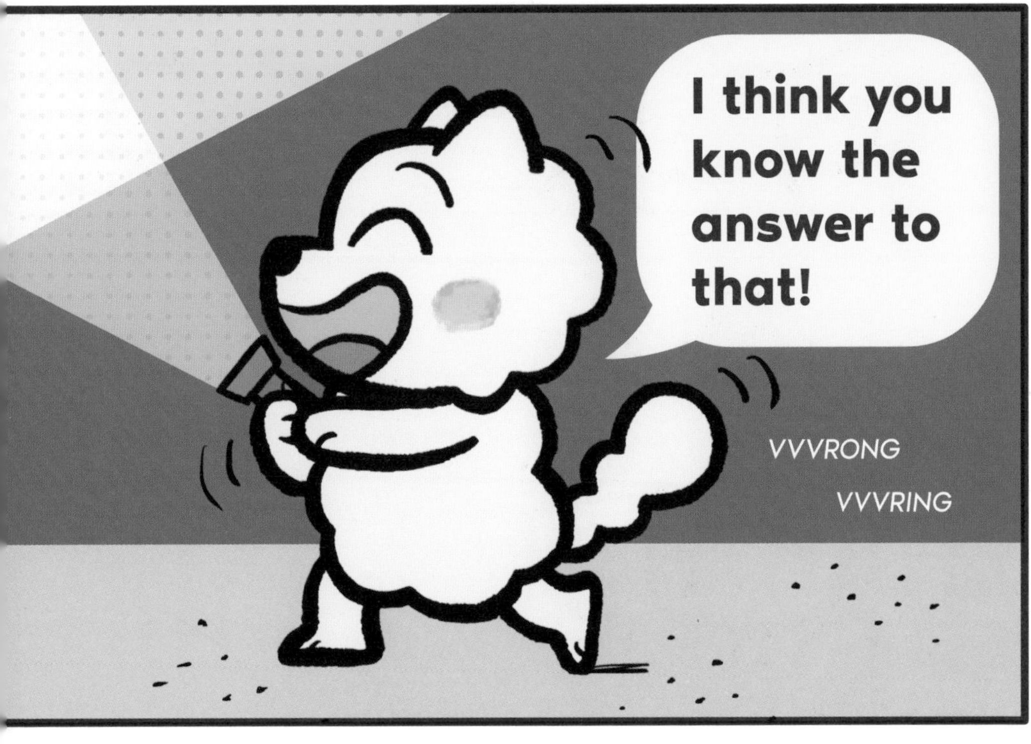
I think you know the answer to that!
VVVRONG
VVVRING

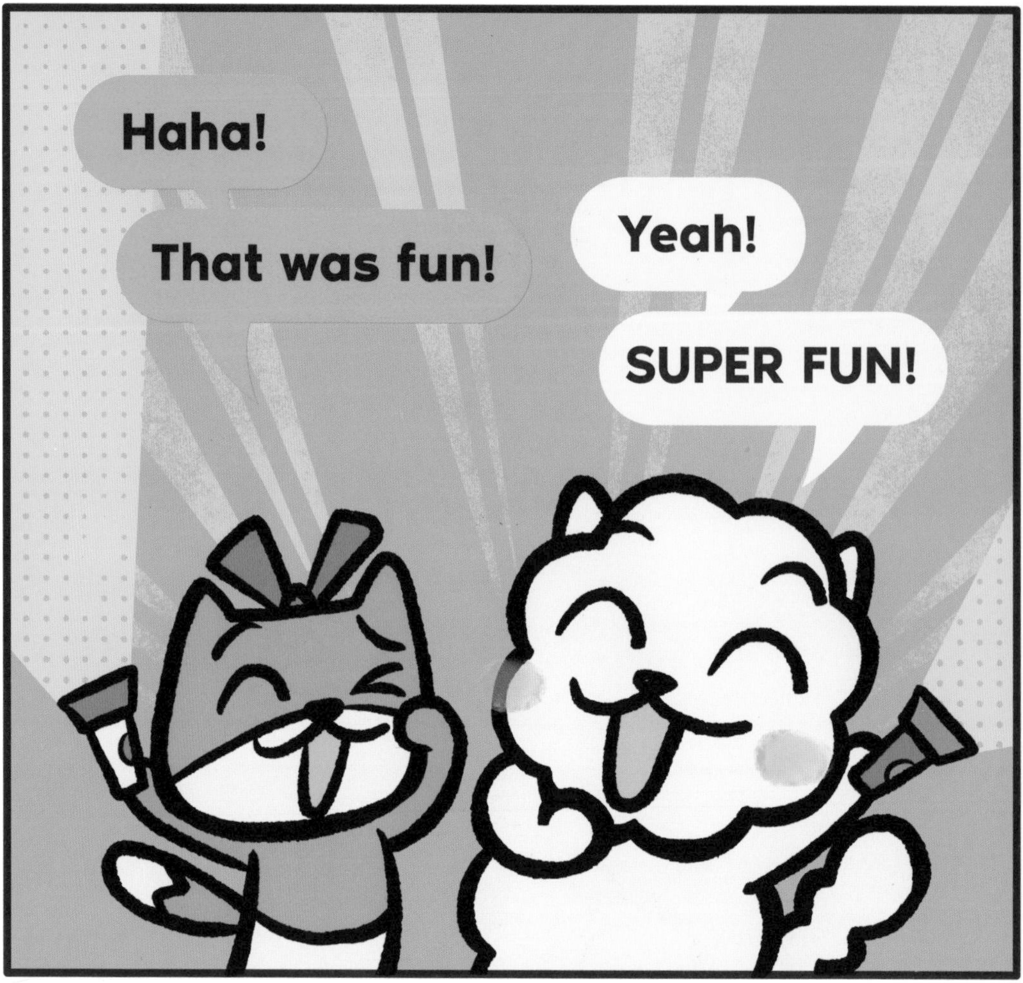
Haha!
That was fun!
Yeah!
SUPER FUN!

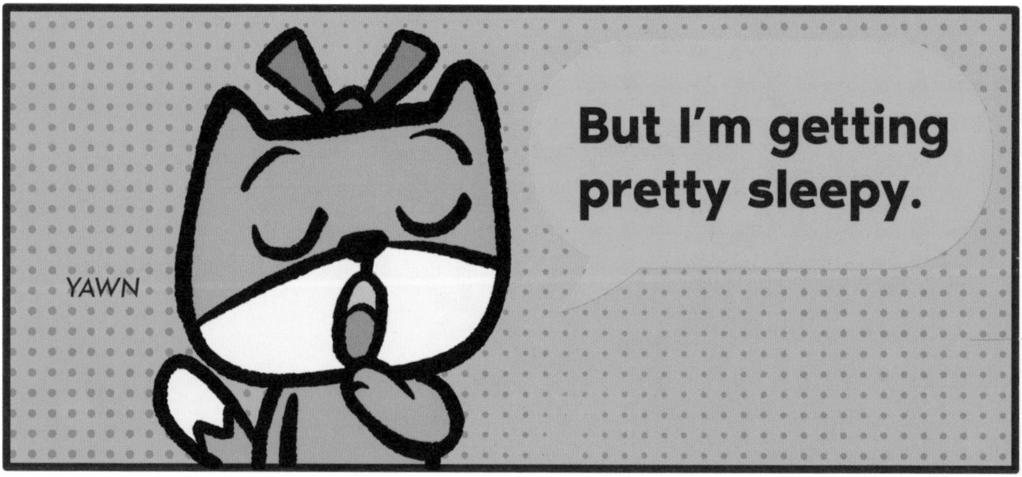
YAWN
But I'm getting pretty sleepy.

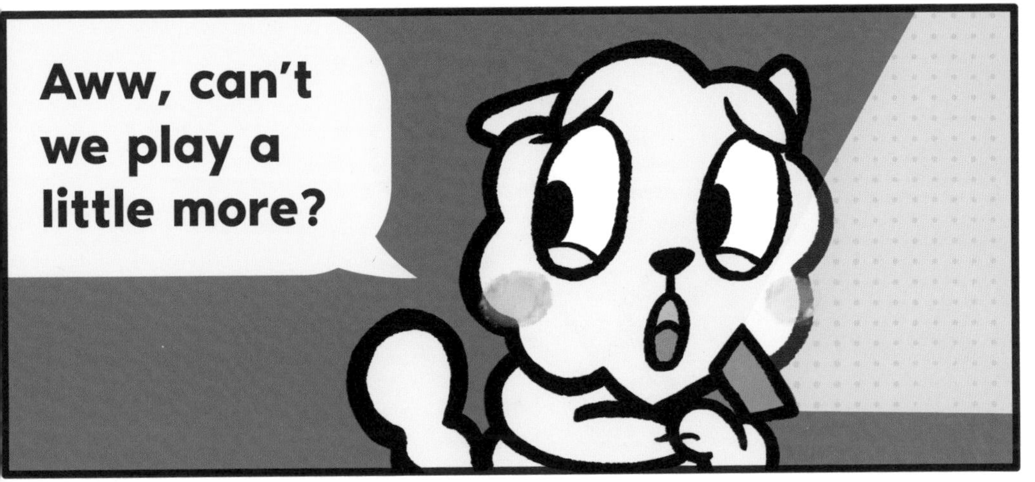
Aww, can't we play a little more?

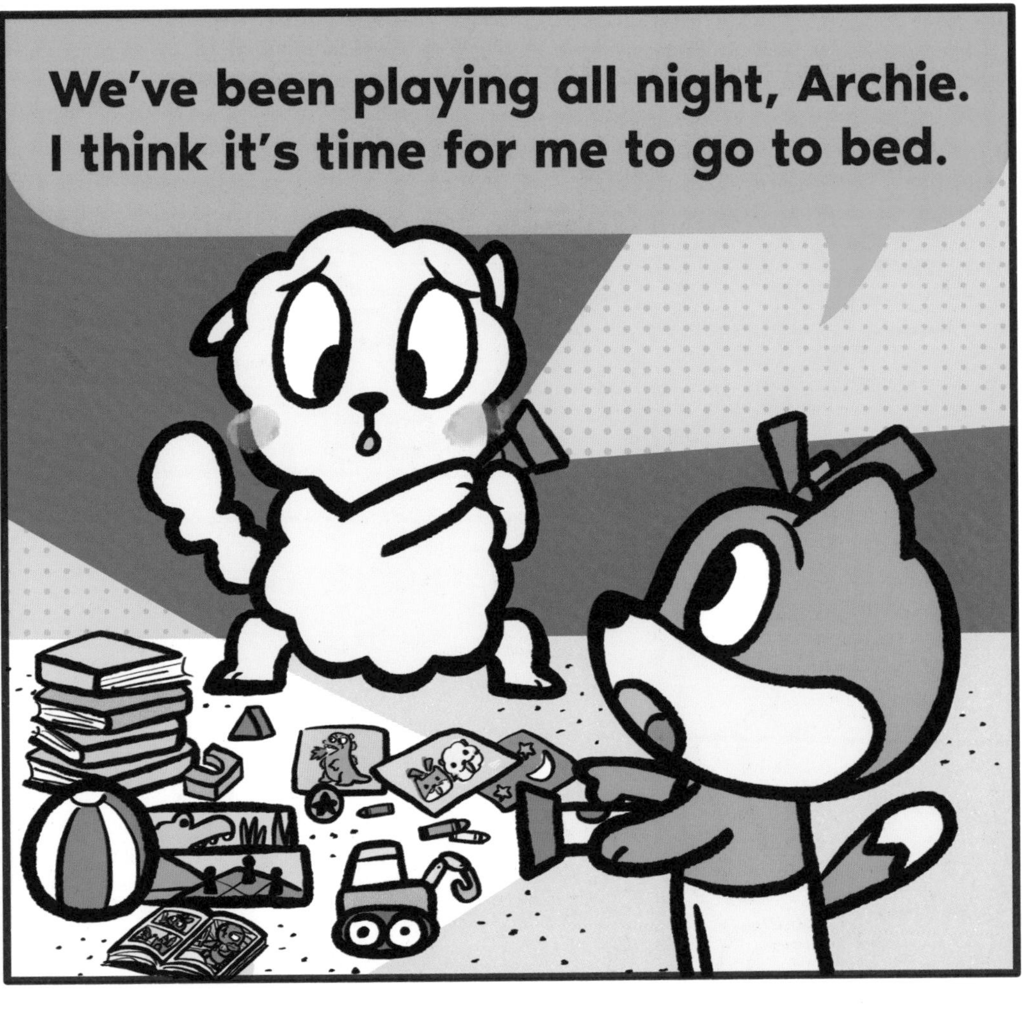
We've been playing all night, Archie. I think it's time for me to go to bed.

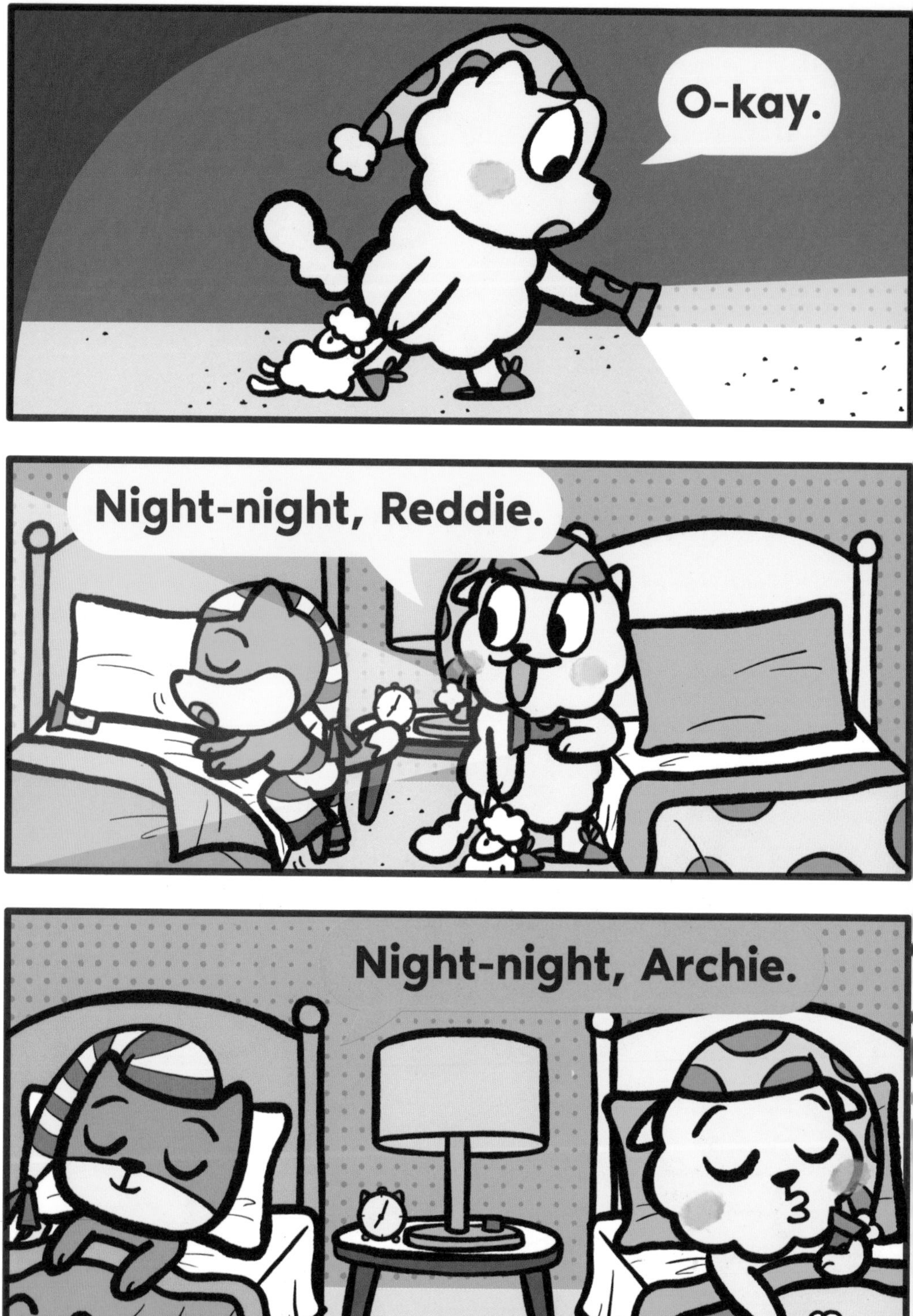
O-kay.
Night-night, Reddie.
Night-night, Archie.

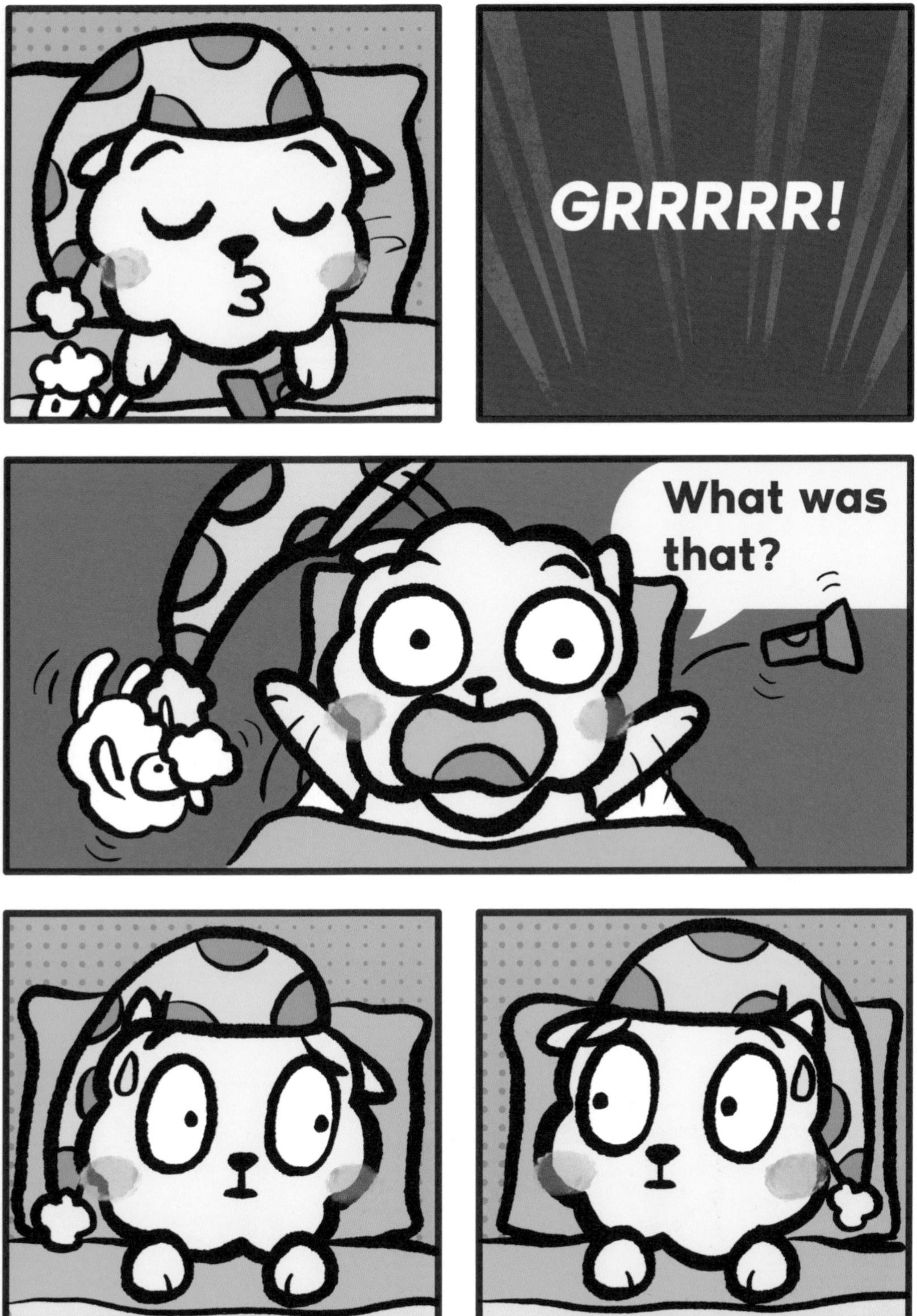
GRRRRR!
What was that?

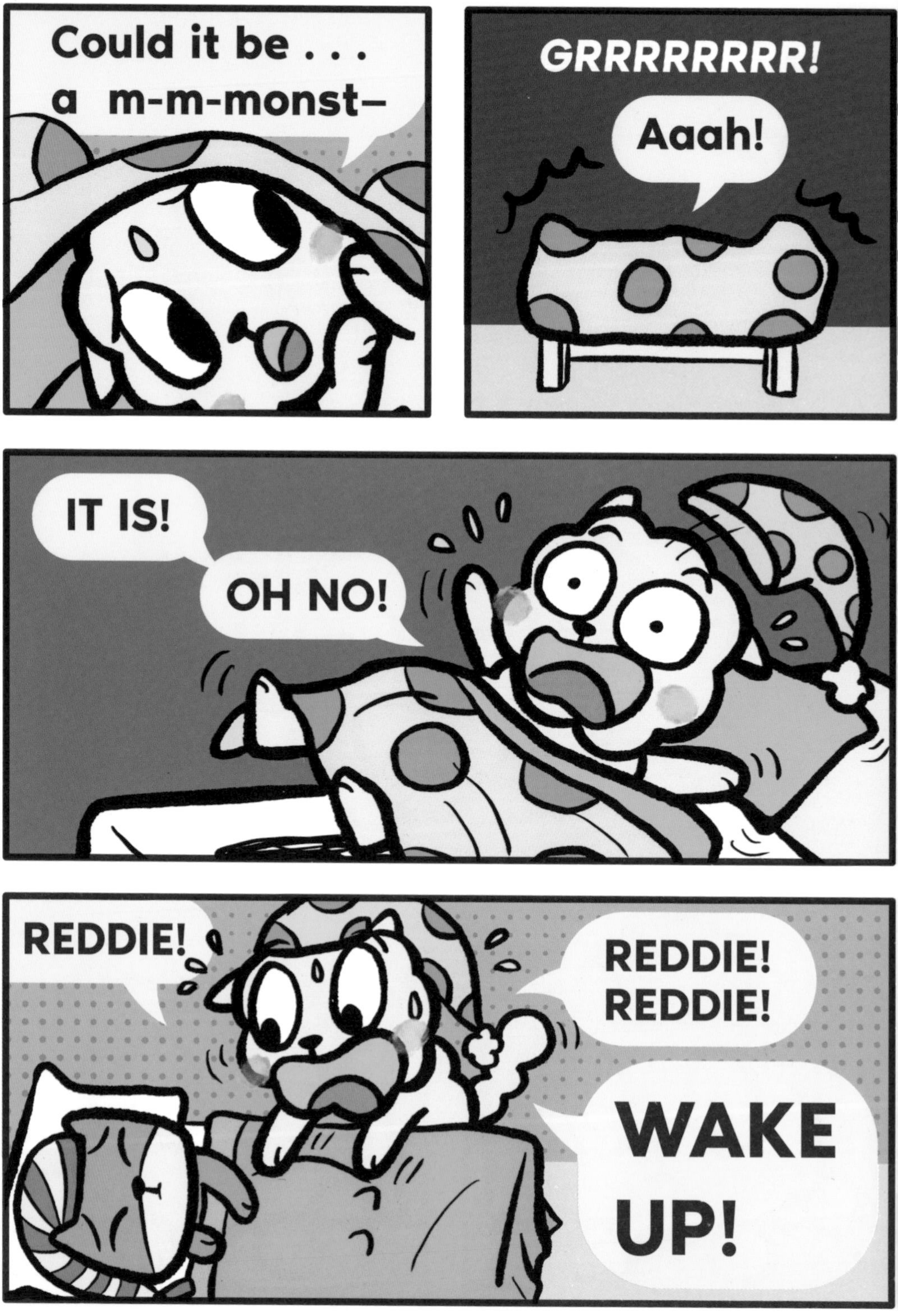
Could it be . . . a m-m-monst–
GRRRRRRRR!
Aaah!
IT IS!
OH NO!
REDDIE!
REDDIE! REDDIE!
WAKE UP!

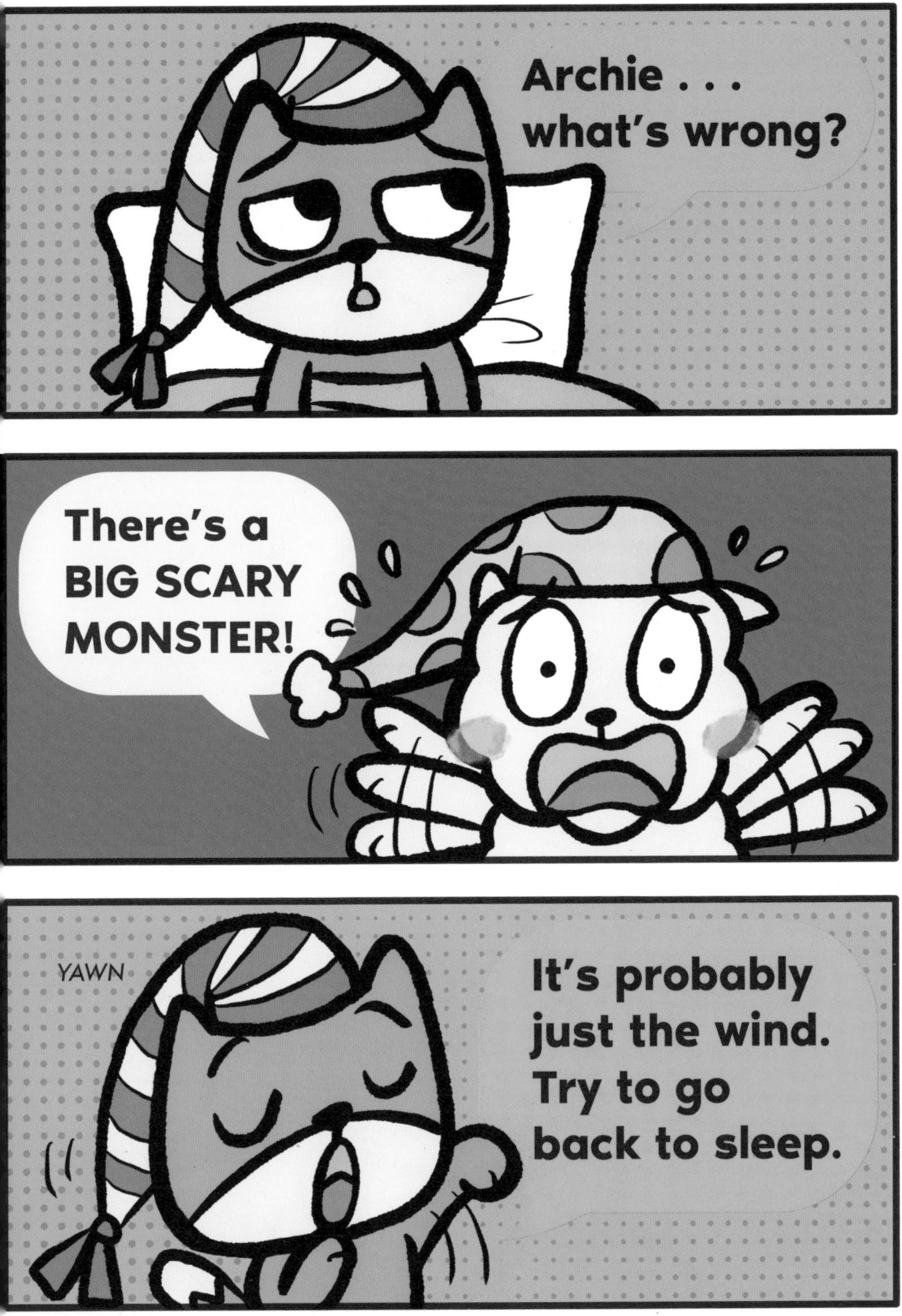
Archie . . . what's wrong?
There's a BIG SCARY MONSTER!
YAWN
It's probably just the wind. Try to go back to sleep.

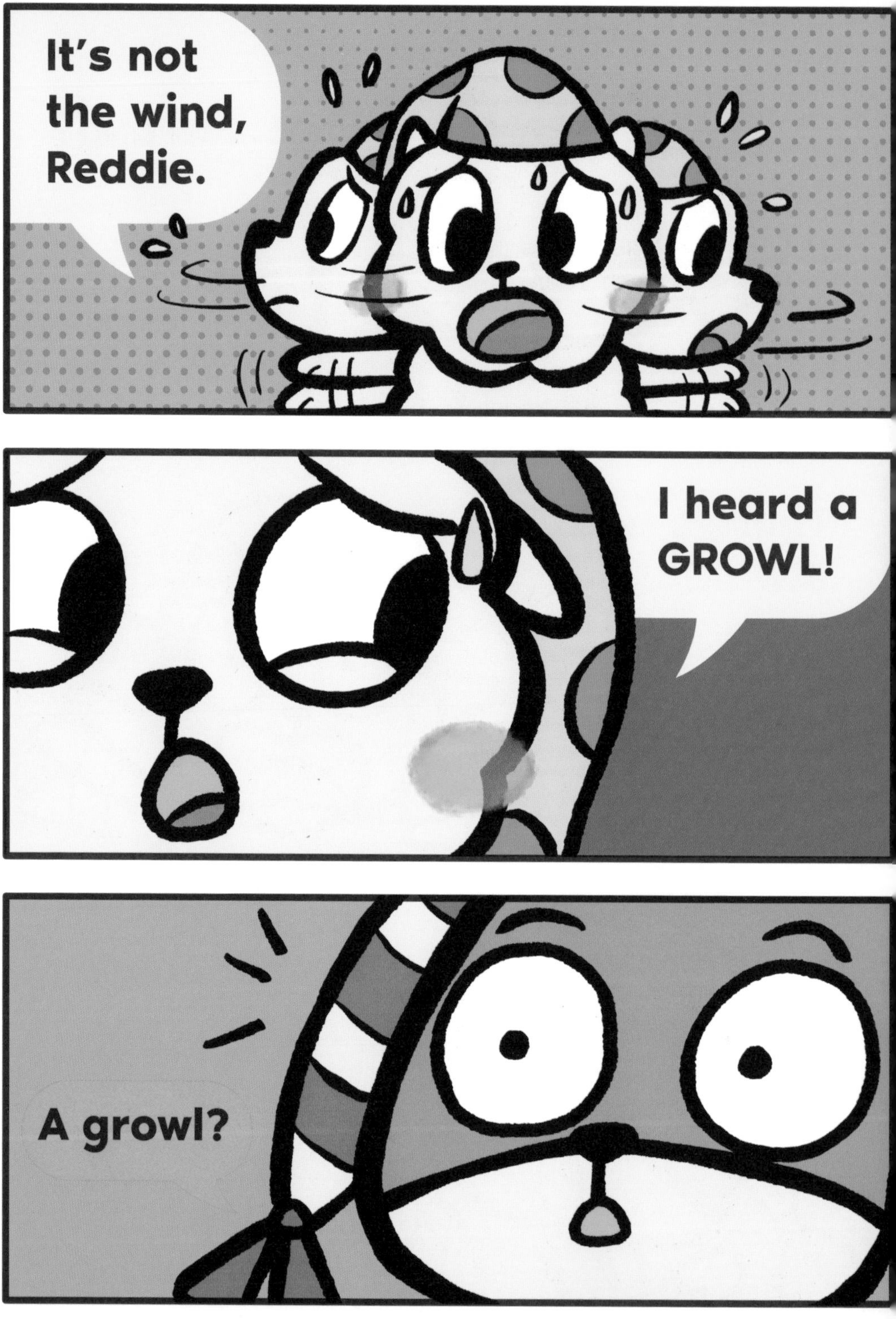
It's not the wind, Reddie.
I heard a GROWL!
A growl?

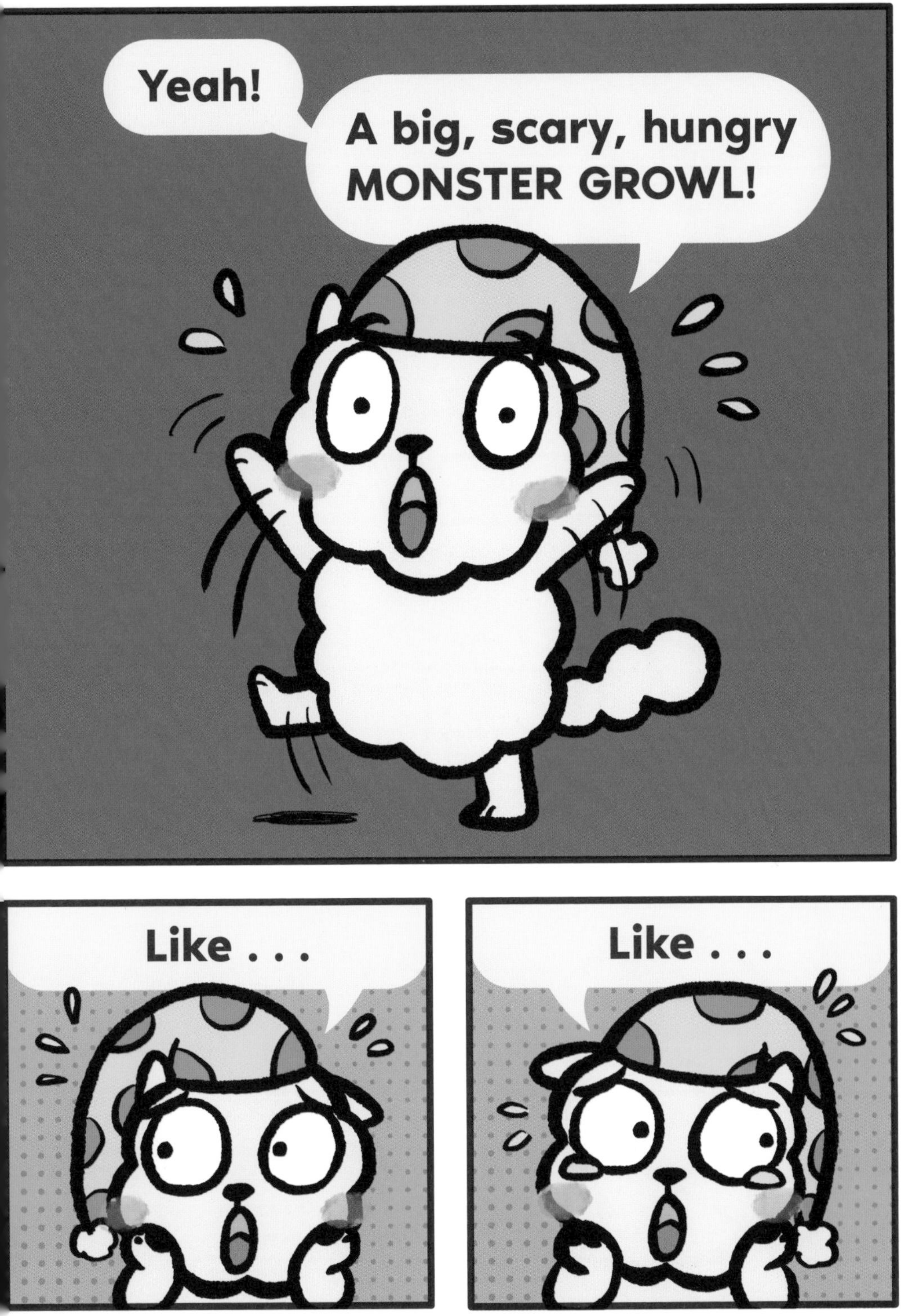
Yeah!
A big, scary, hungry MONSTER GROWL!
Like . . .
Like . . .

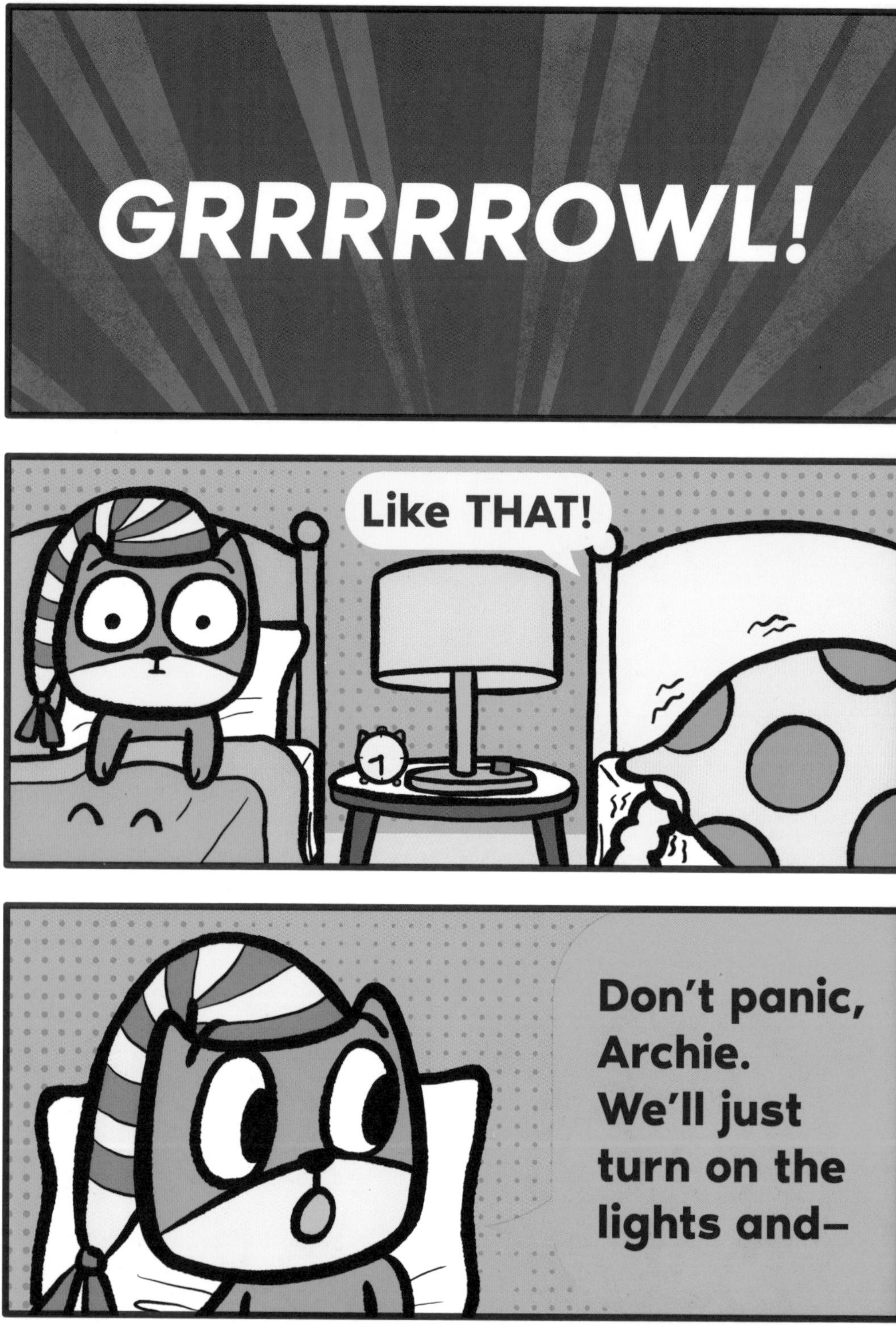
GRRRRRROWL!
Like THAT!
Don't panic, Archie. We'll just turn on the lights and–

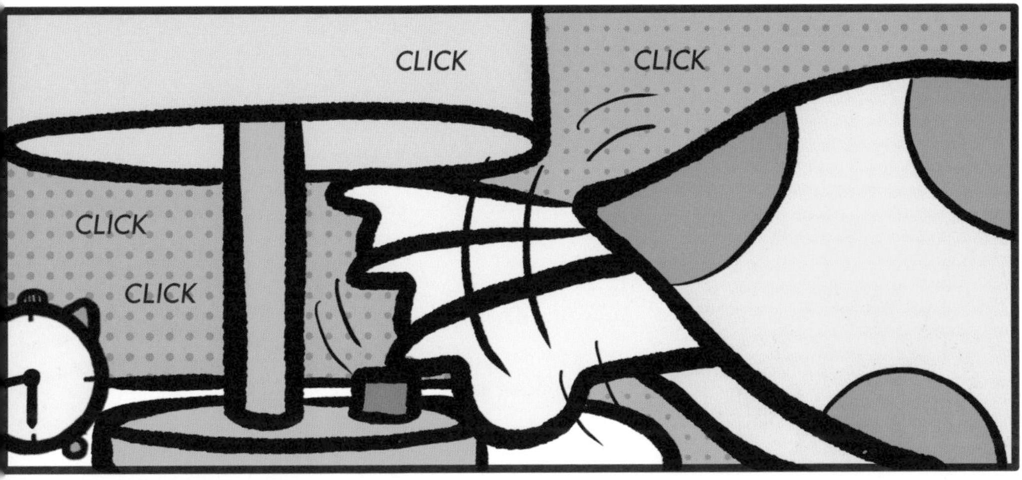
CLICK
CLICK
CLICK
CLICK

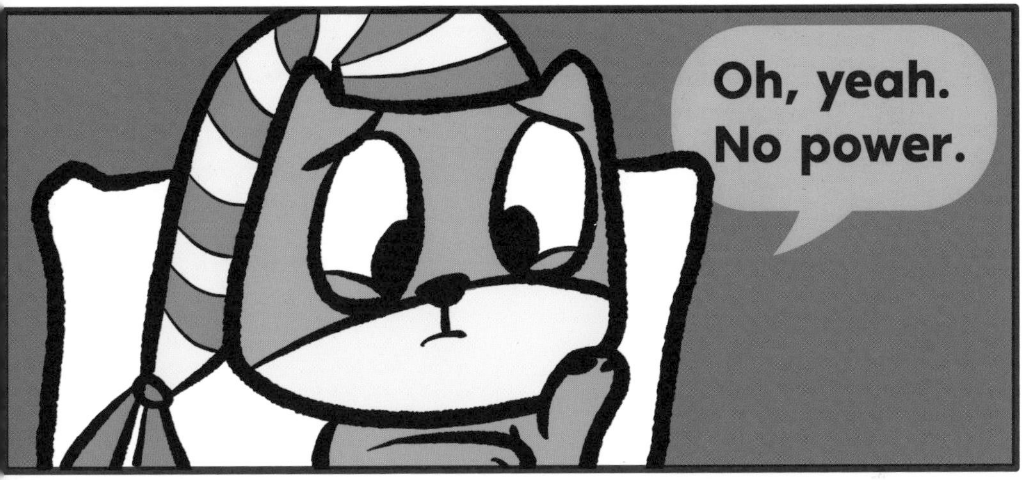
Oh, yeah. No power.

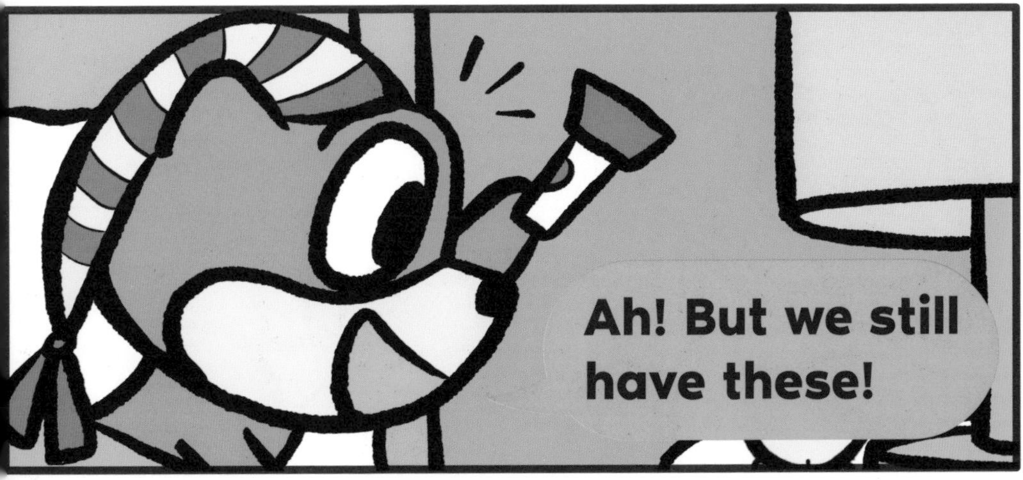
Ah! But we still have these!

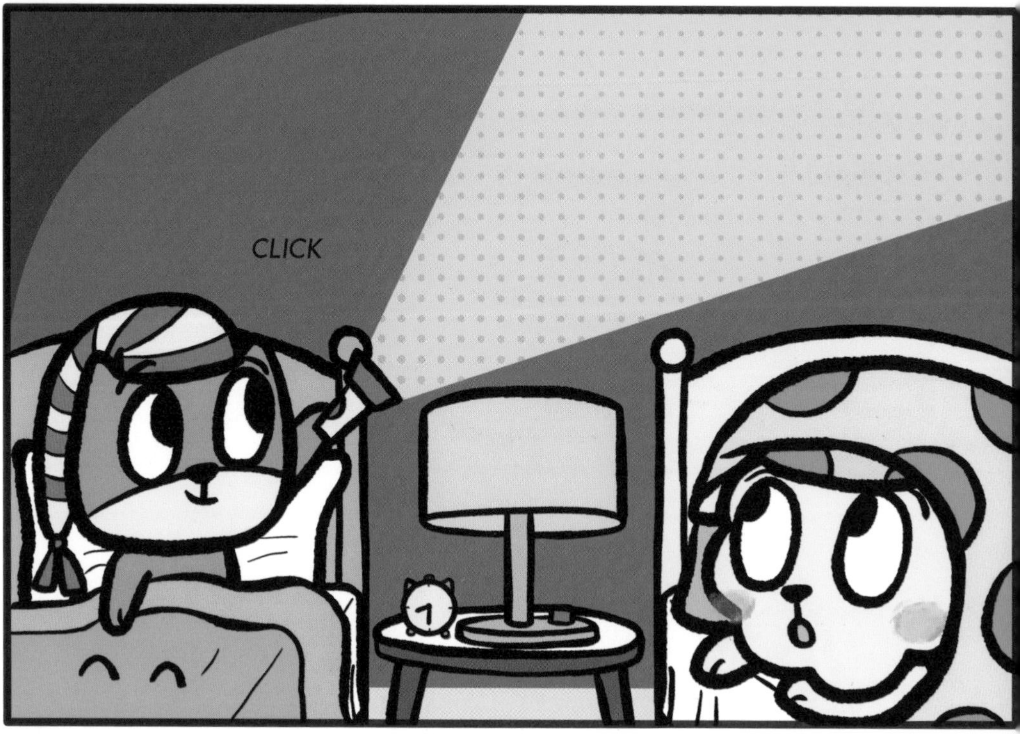
CLICK

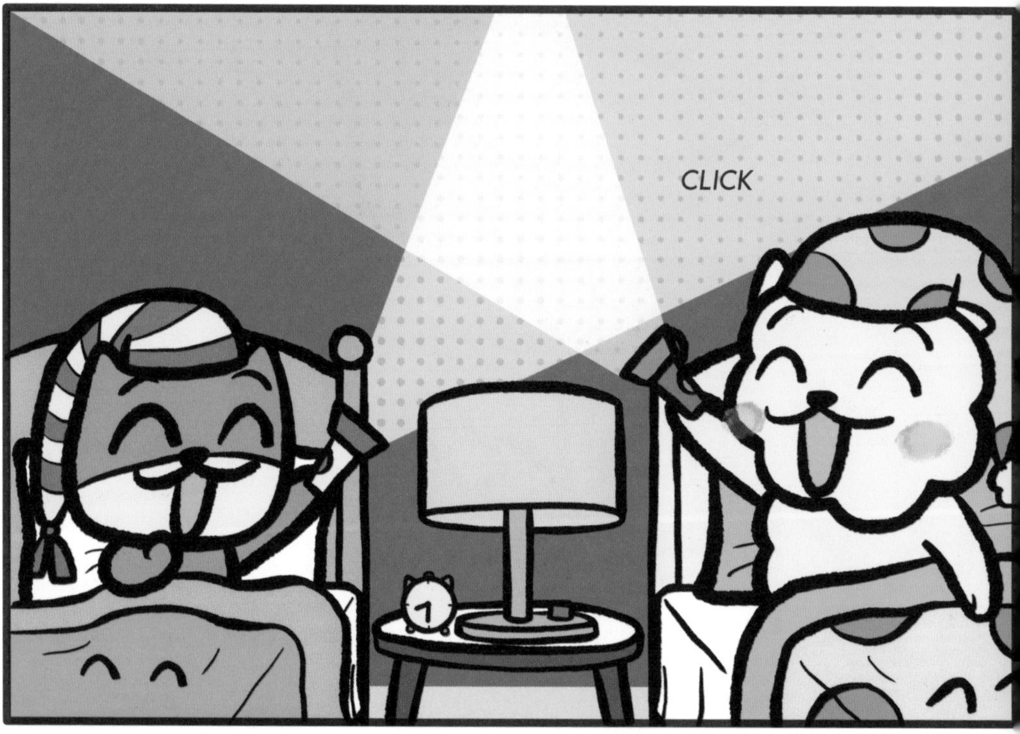
CLICK

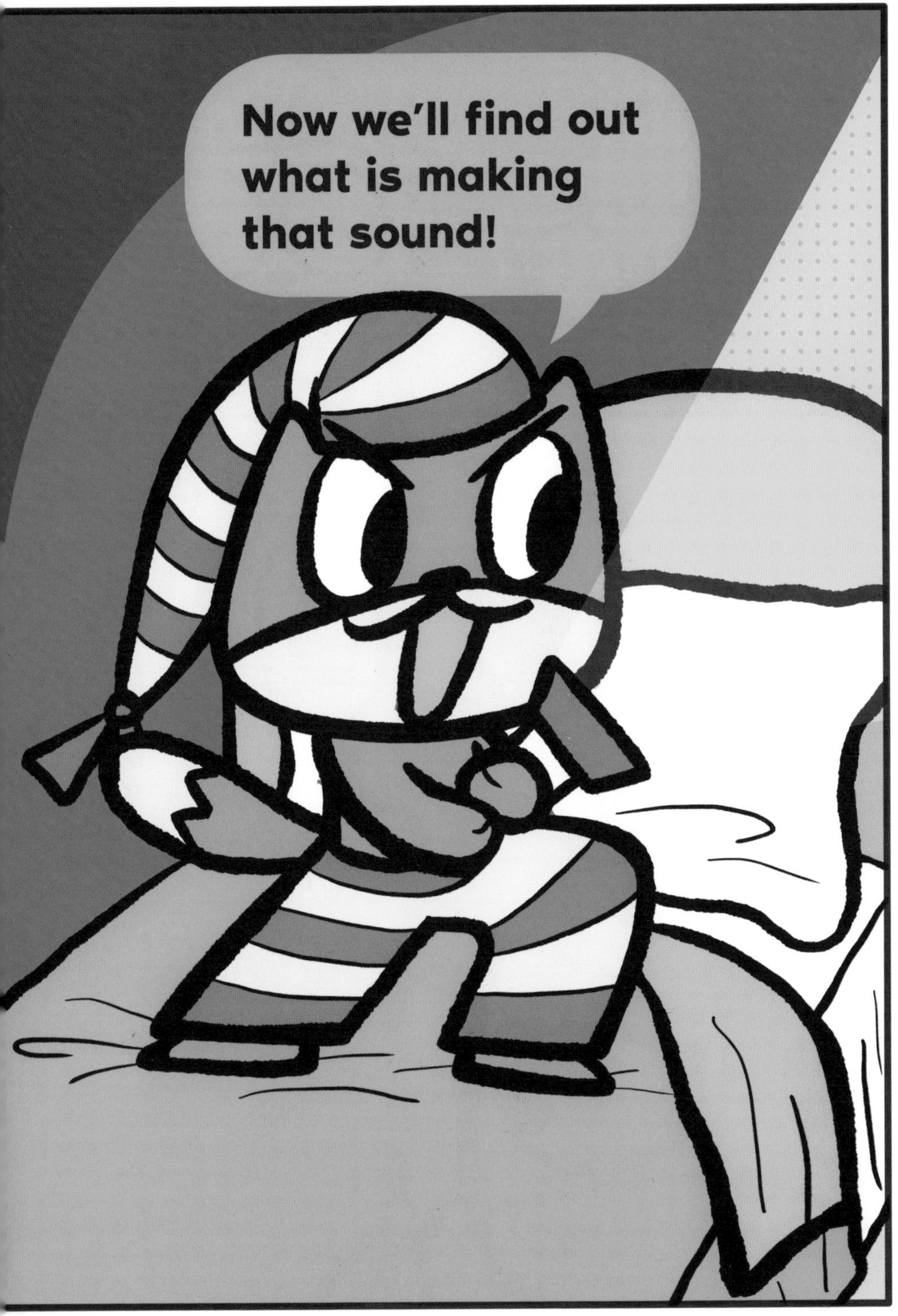
Now we'll find out what is making that sound!

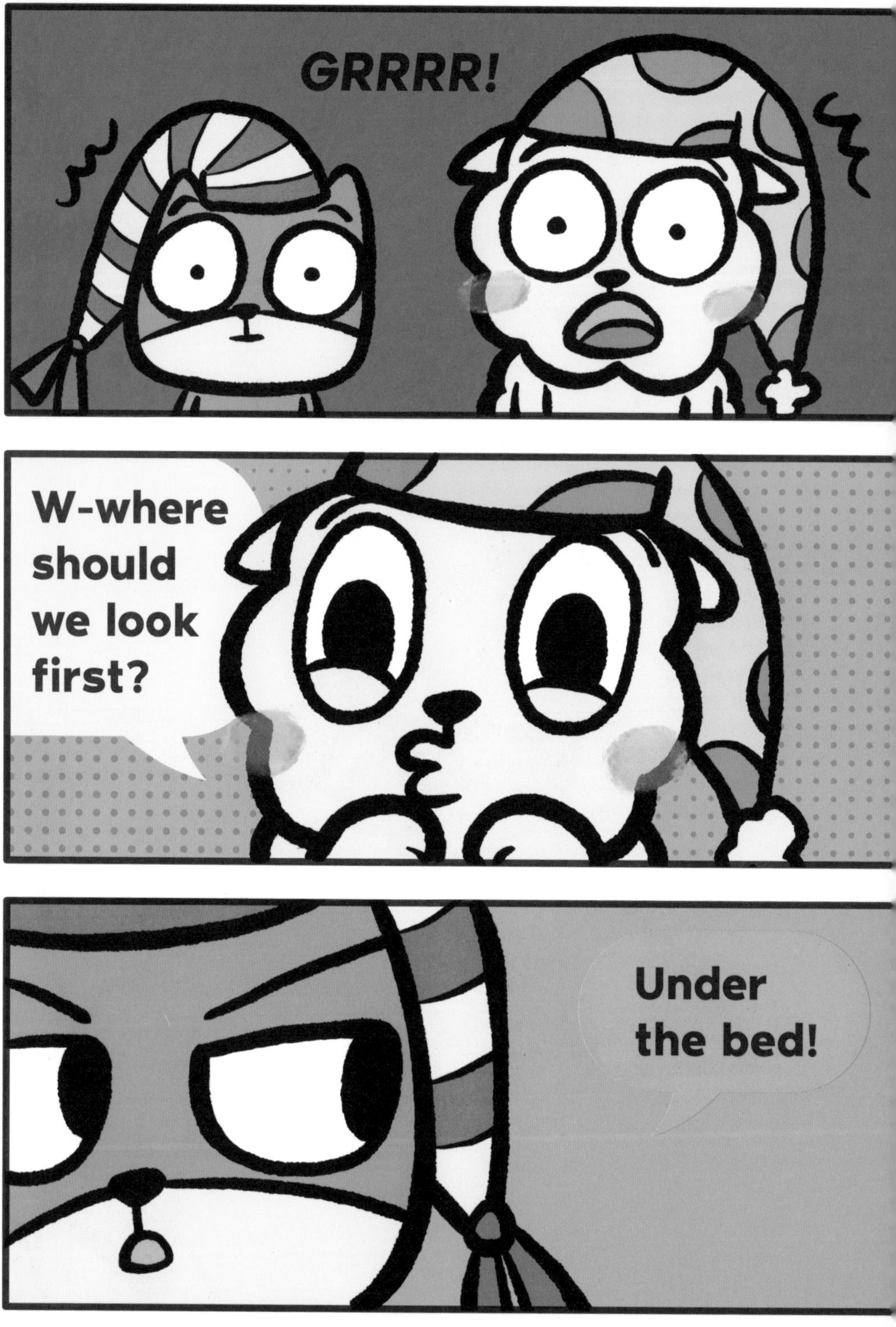
GRRRR!
W-where should we look first?
Under the bed!

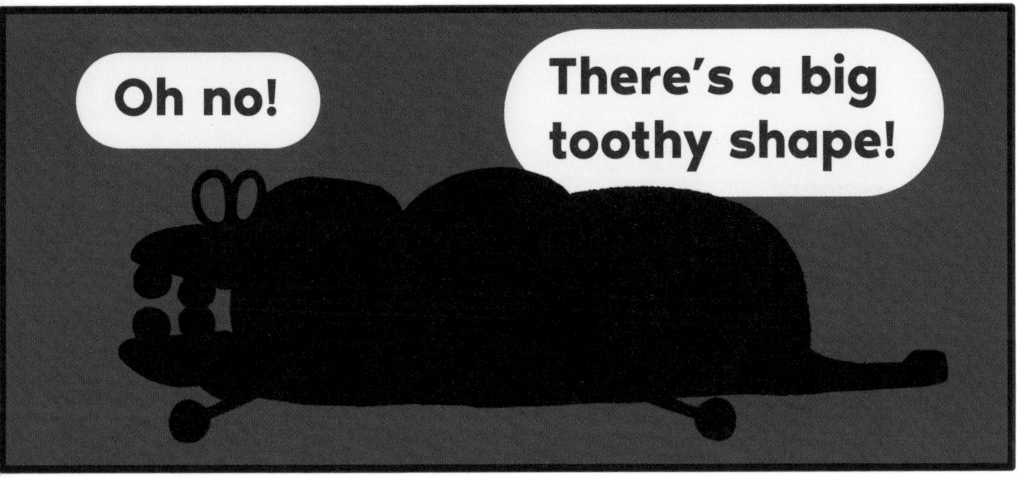
Oh no!
There's a big toothy shape!

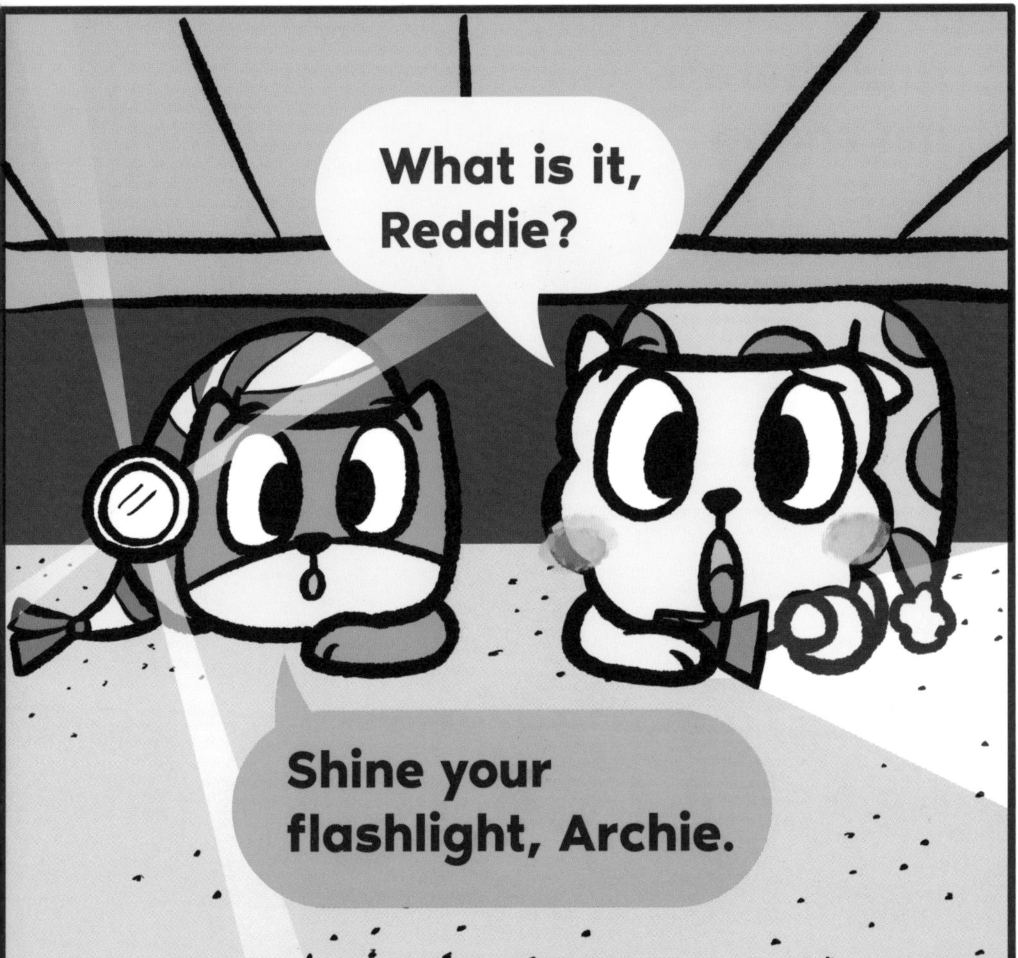
What is it, Reddie?
Shine your flashlight, Archie.

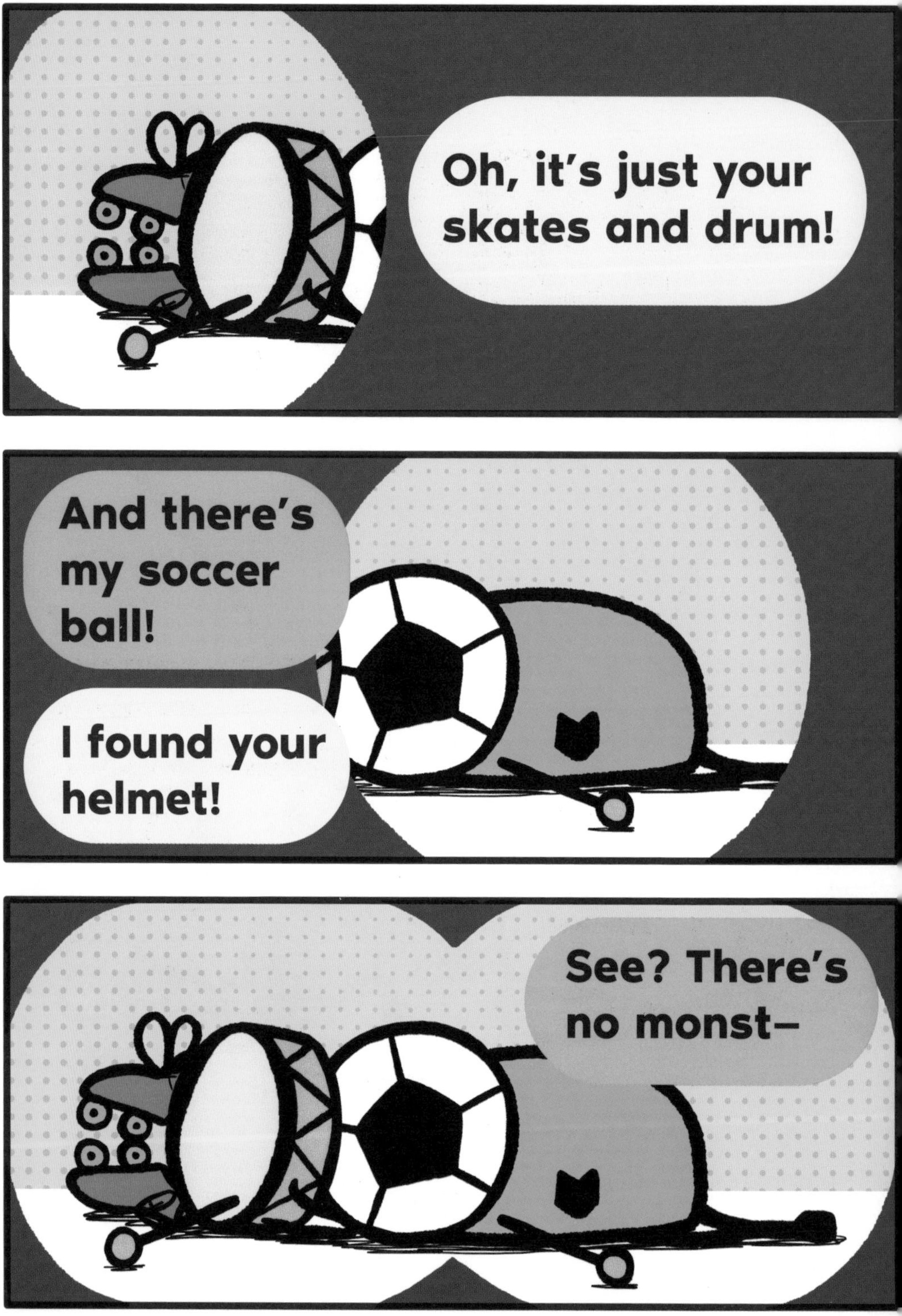
Oh, it's just your skates and drum!
And there's my soccer ball!
I found your helmet!
See? There's no monst–

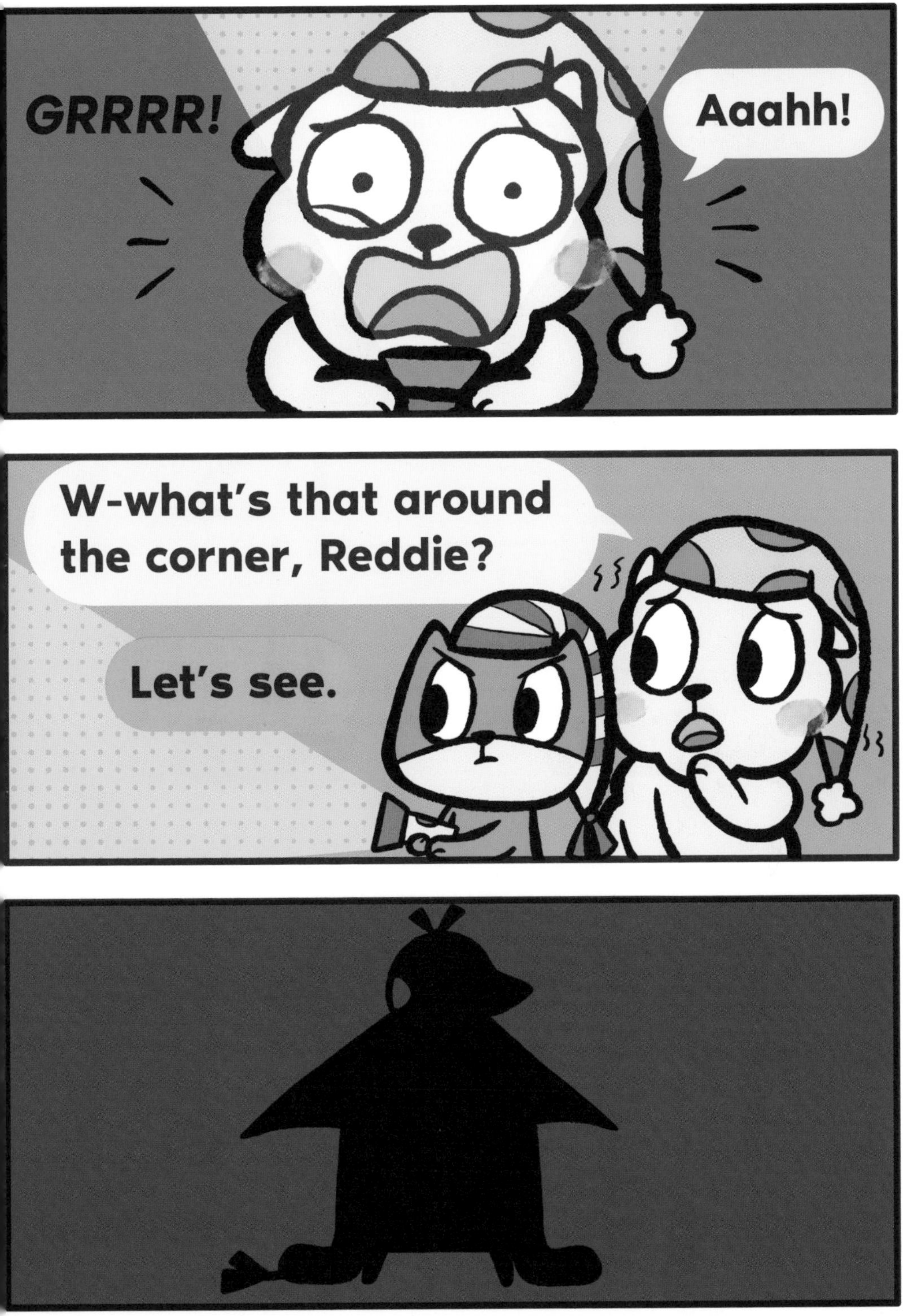
GRRRR!
Aaahh!
W-what's that around the corner, Reddie?
Let's see.

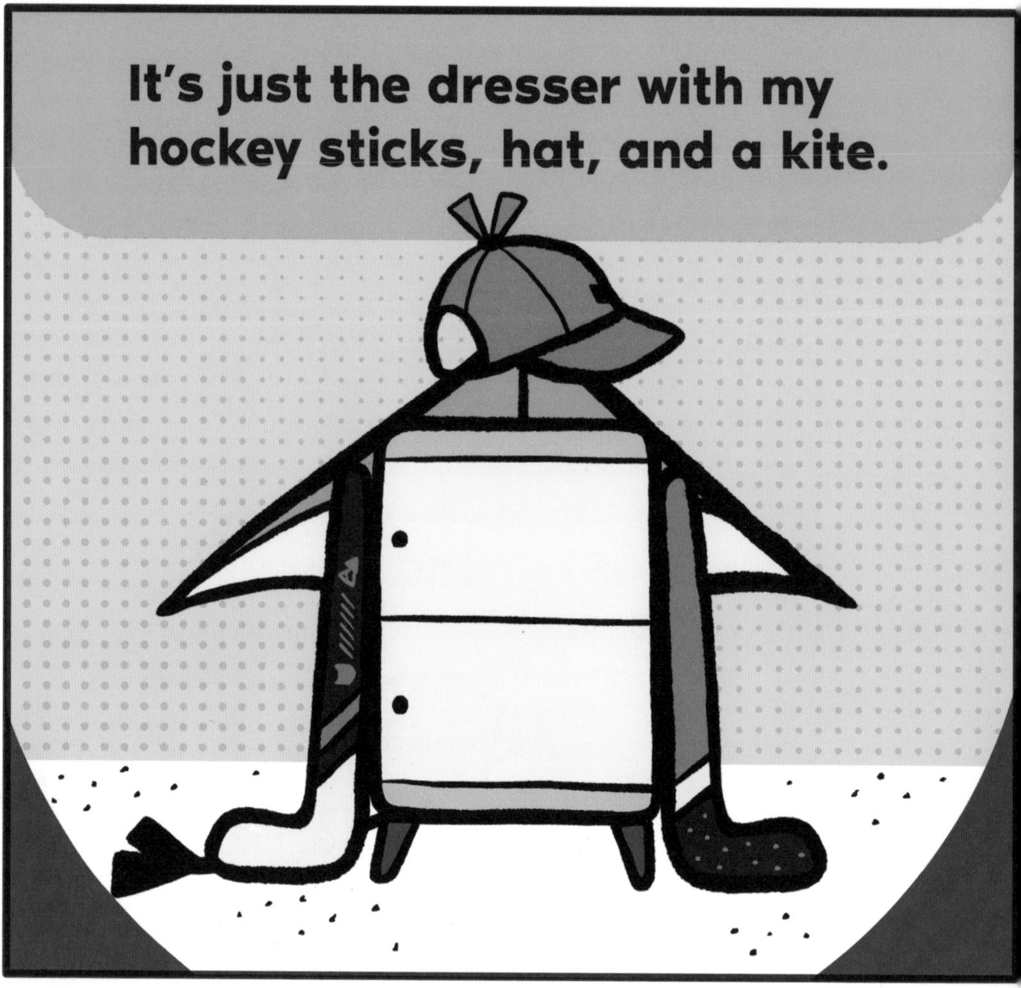
It's just the dresser with my hockey sticks, hat, and a kite.

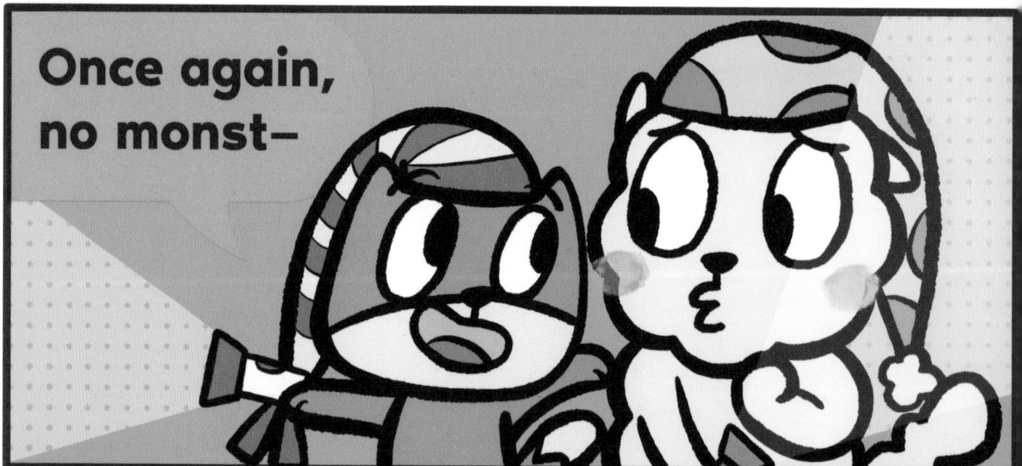
Once again, no monst–

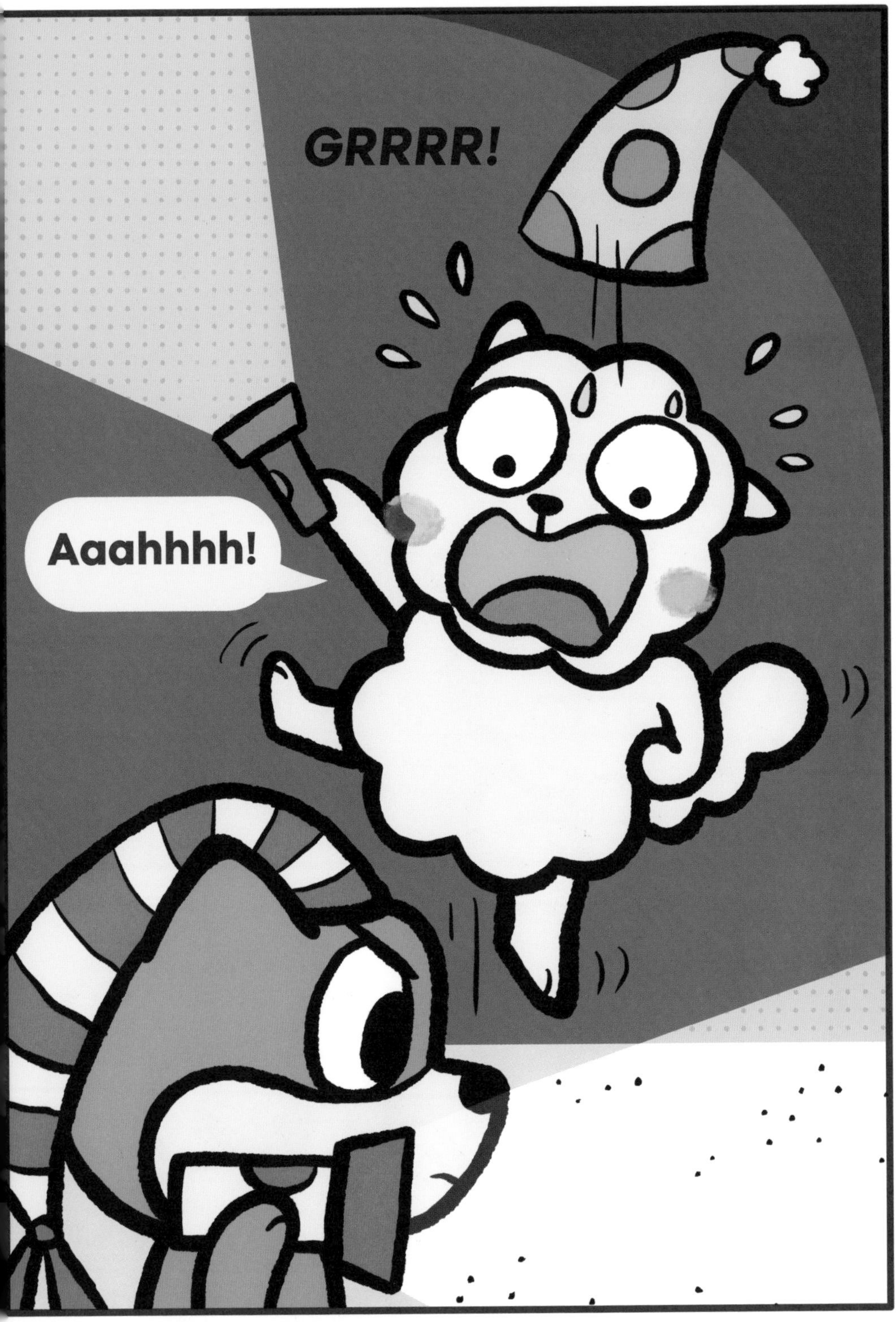
GRRRR!
Aaahhhh!

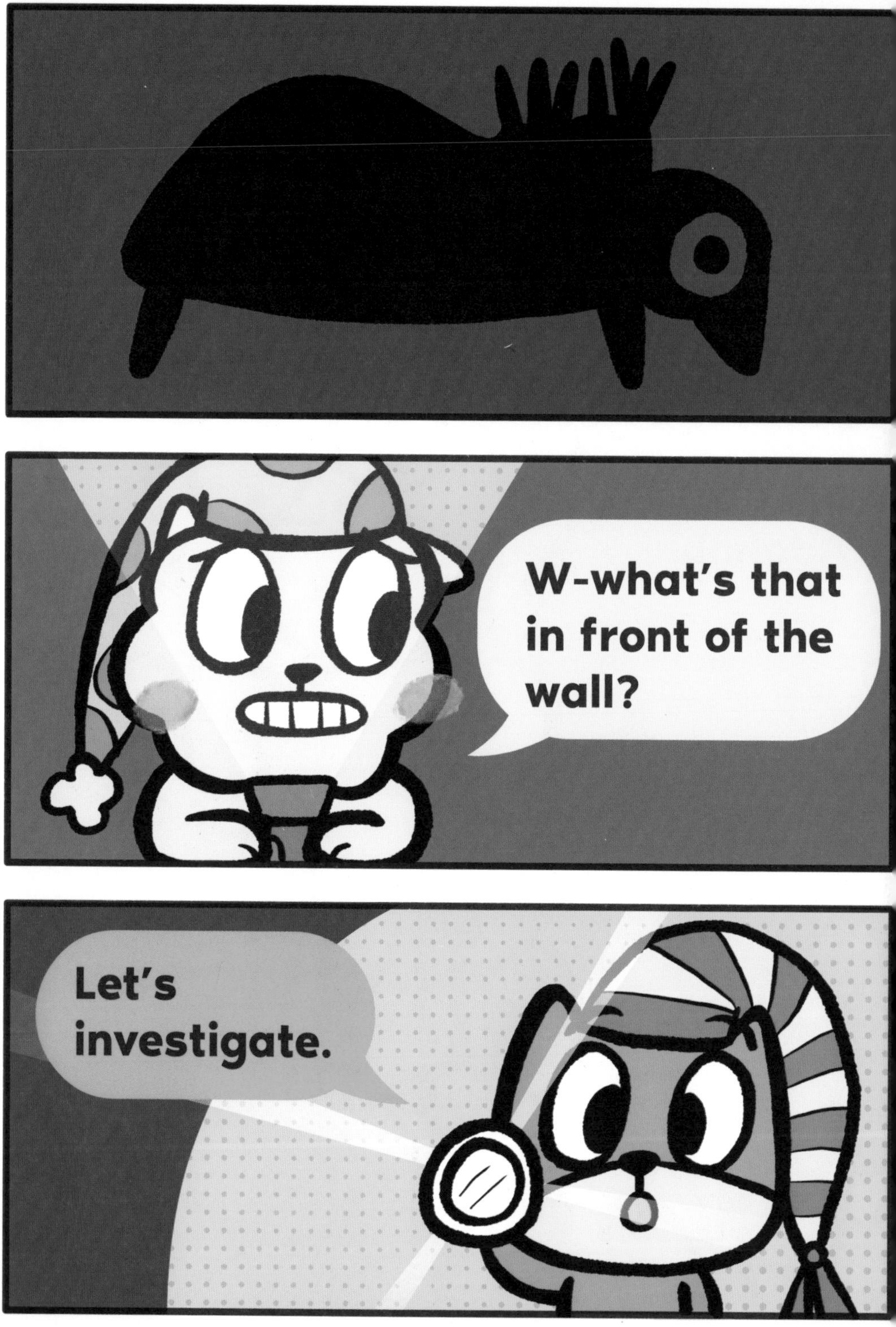
W-what's that in front of the wall?
Let's investigate.

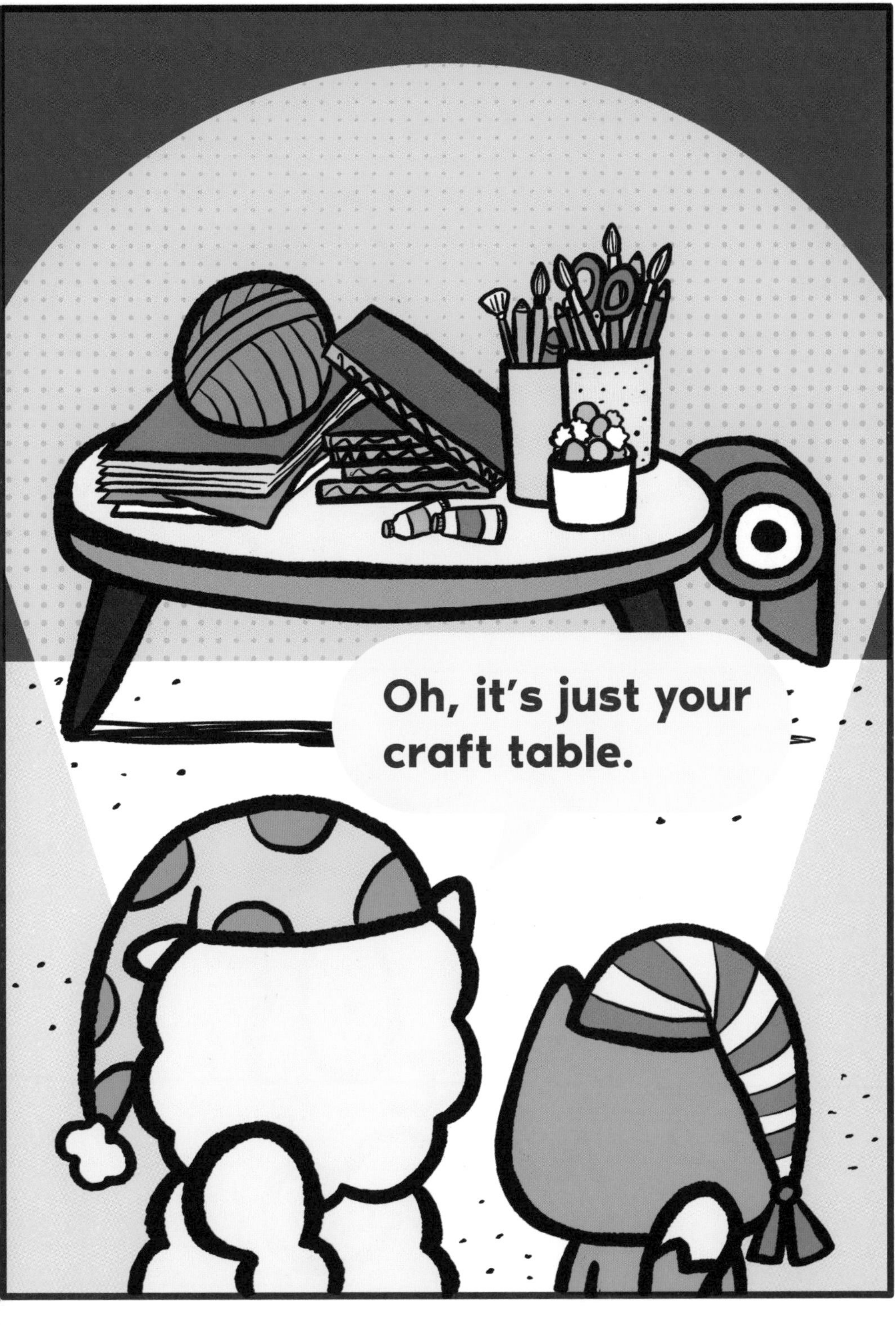
Oh, it's just your craft table.

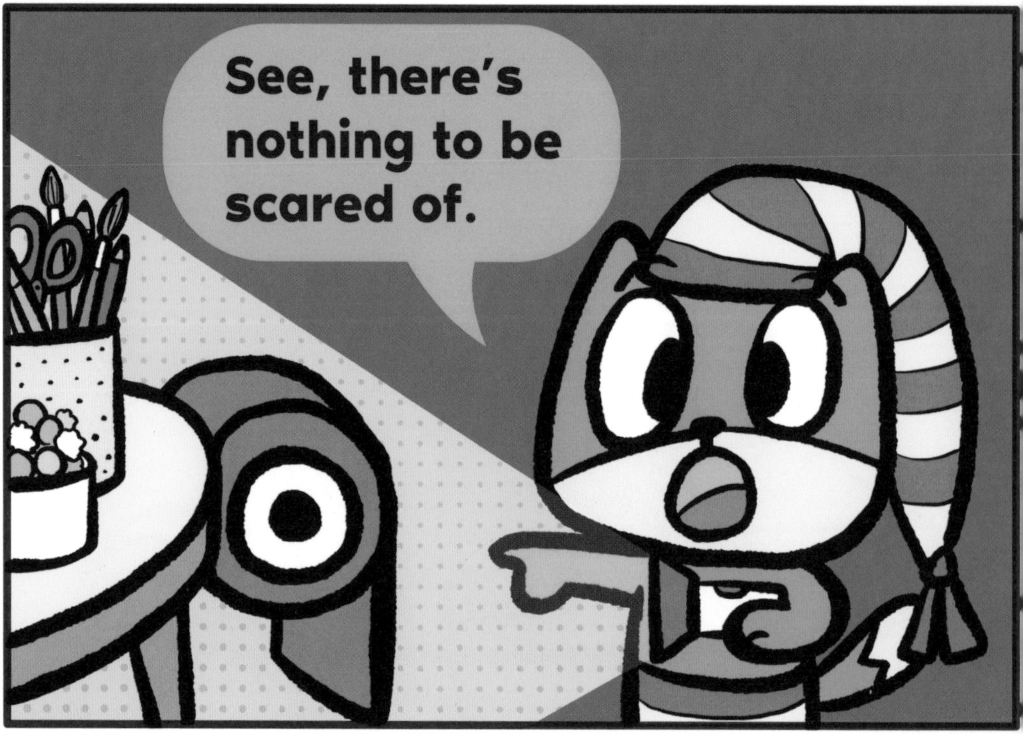
See, there's nothing to be scared of.

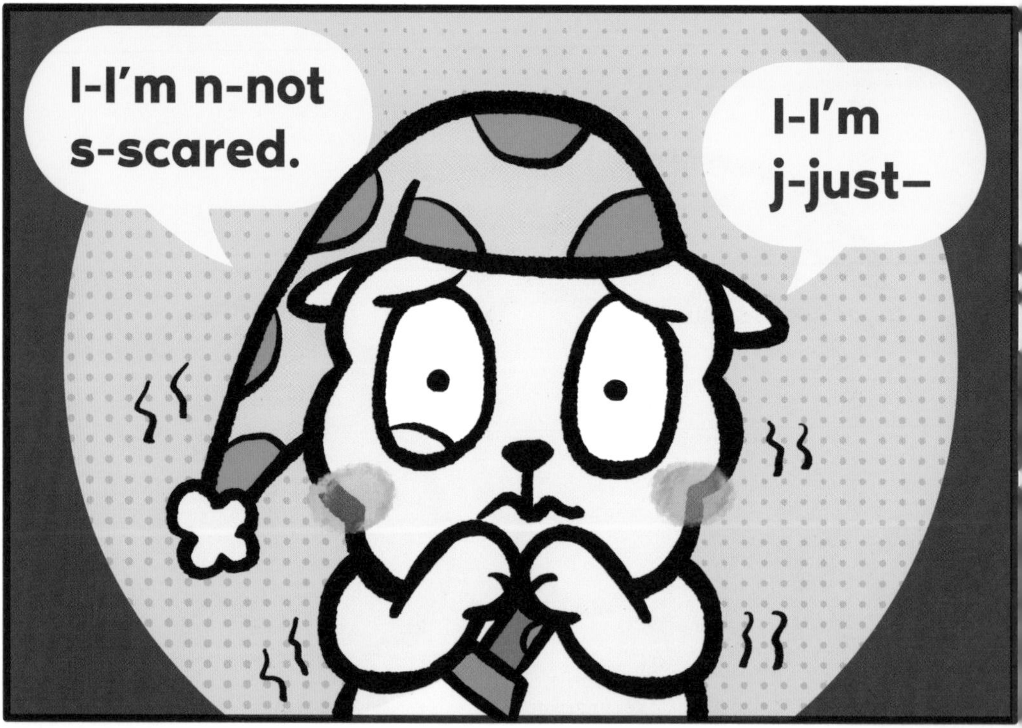
I-I'm n-not s-scared.
I-I'm j-just–

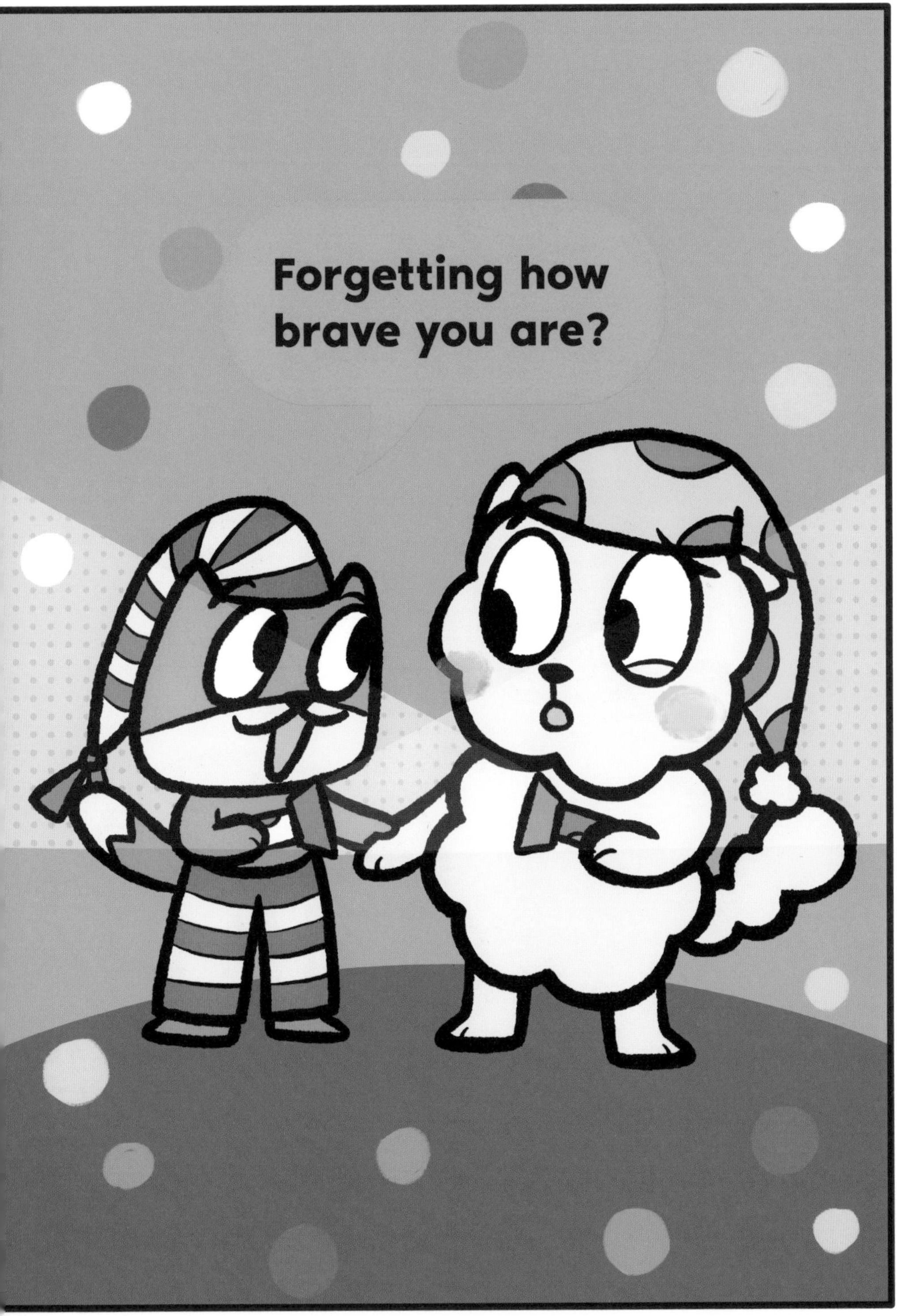
Forgetting how brave you are?

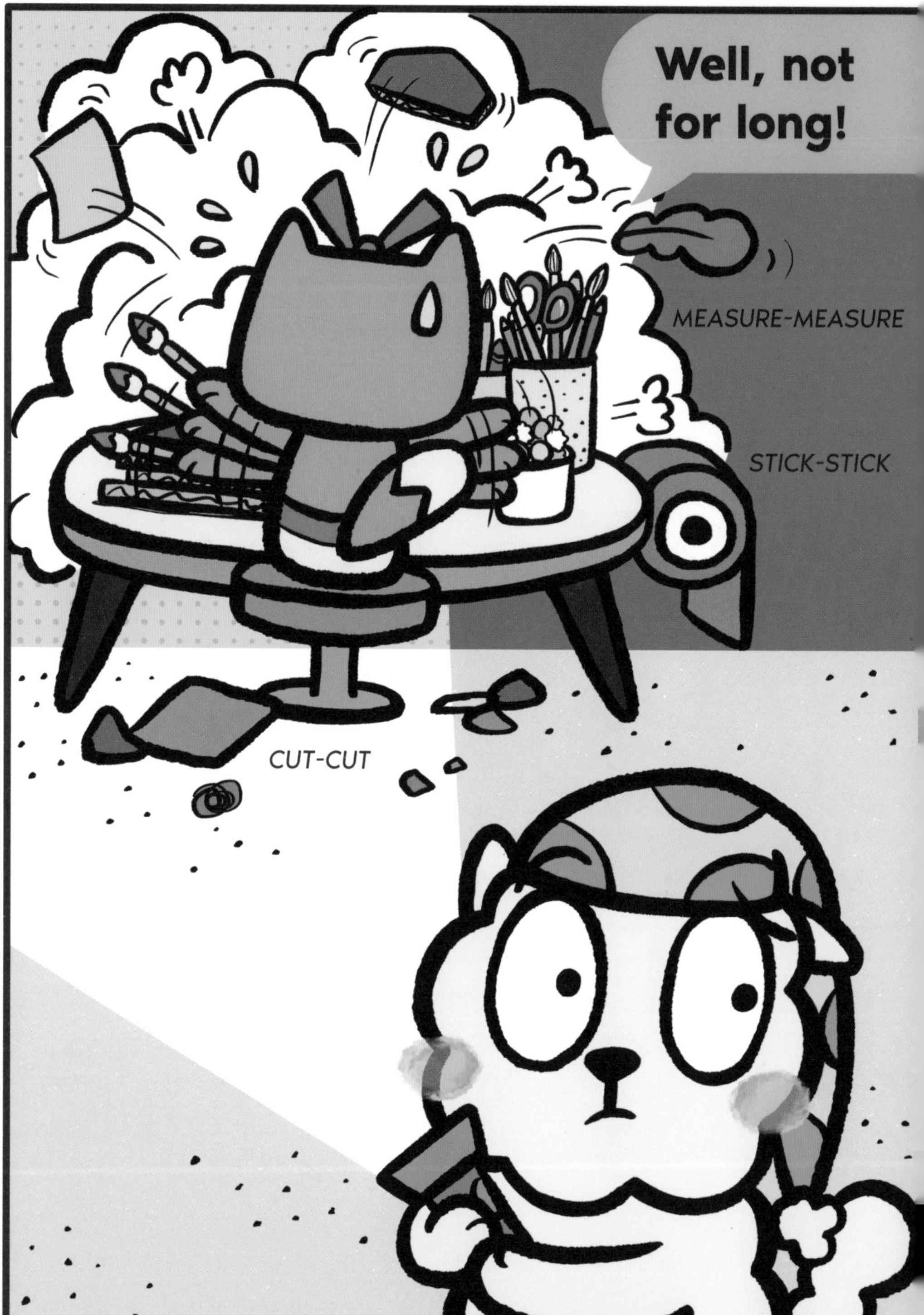
Well, not for long!
MEASURE-MEASURE
STICK-STICK
CUT-CUT

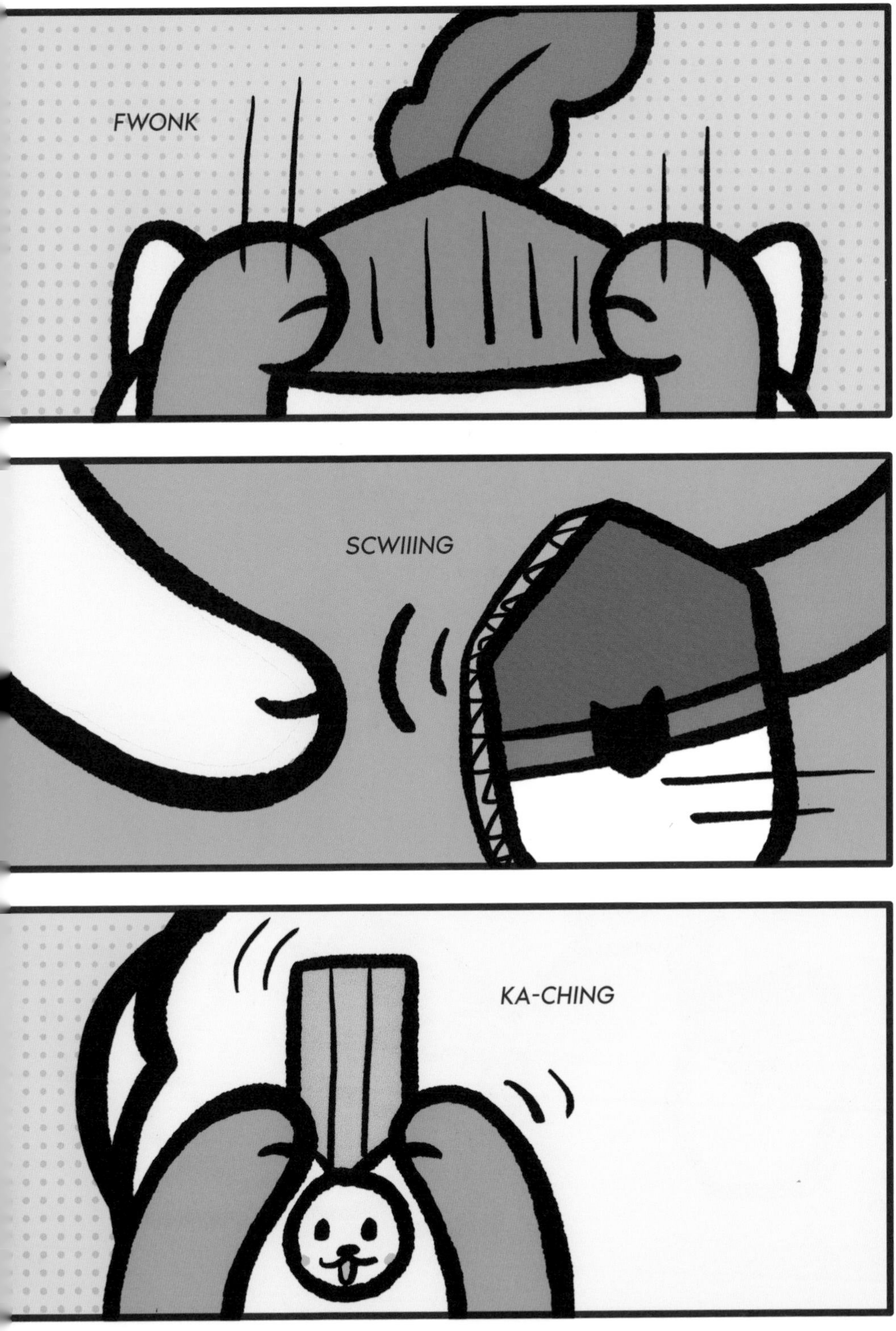
FWONK
SCWIIING
KA-CHING

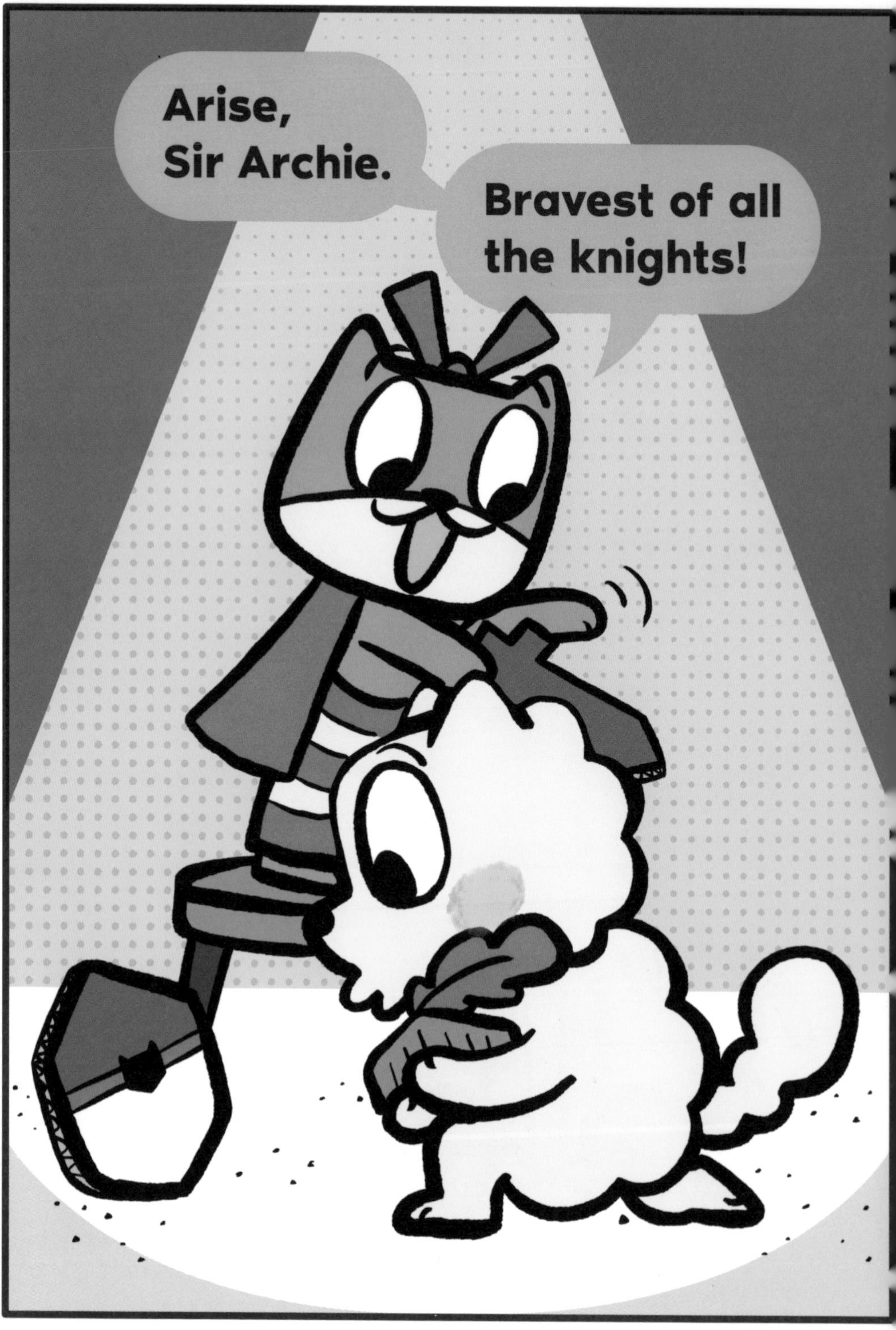
Arise,
Sir Archie.
Bravest of all
the knights!

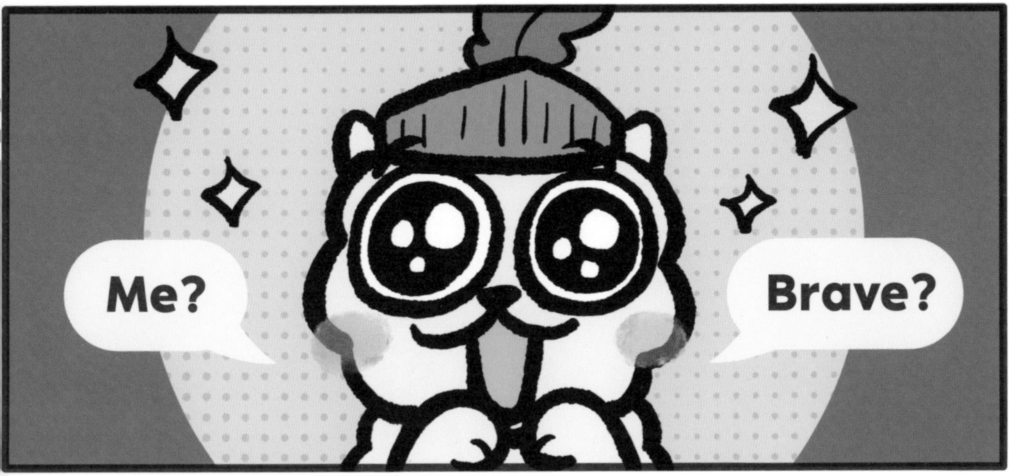
Me?
Brave?

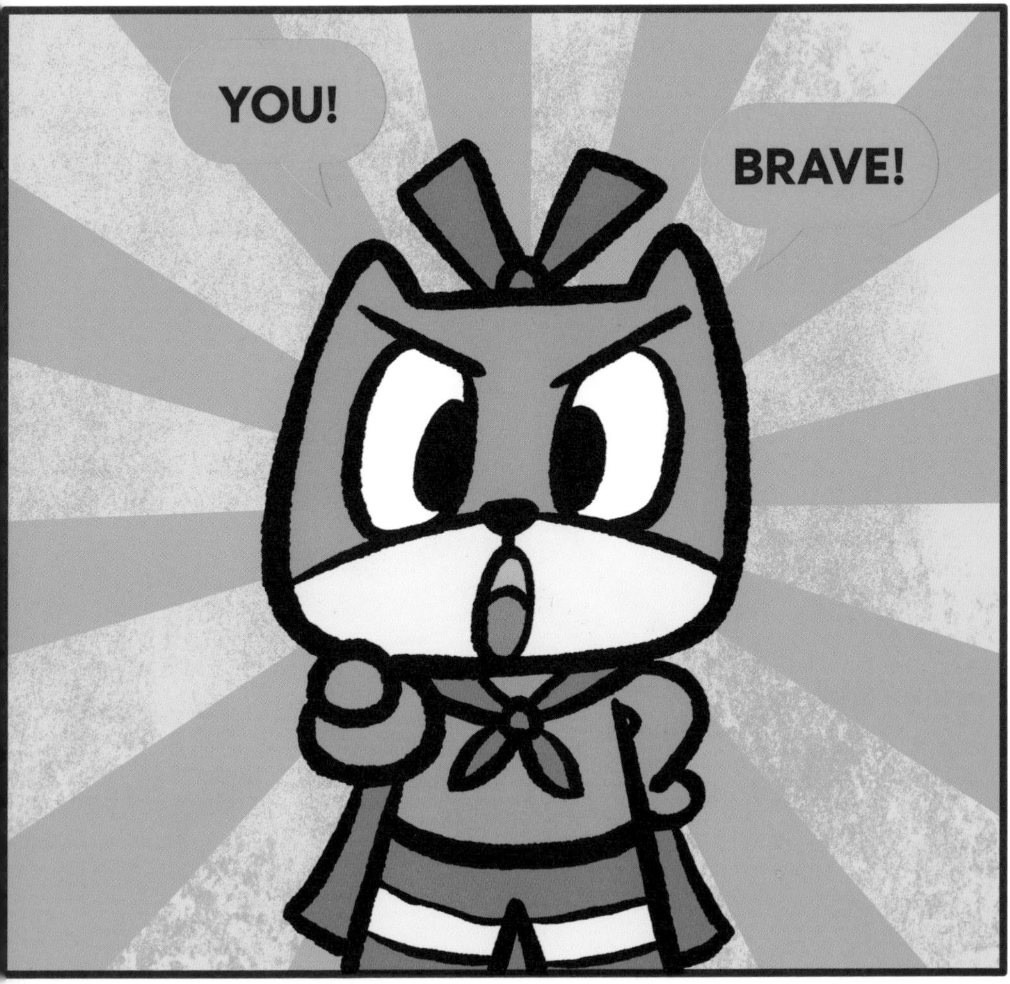
YOU!
BRAVE!

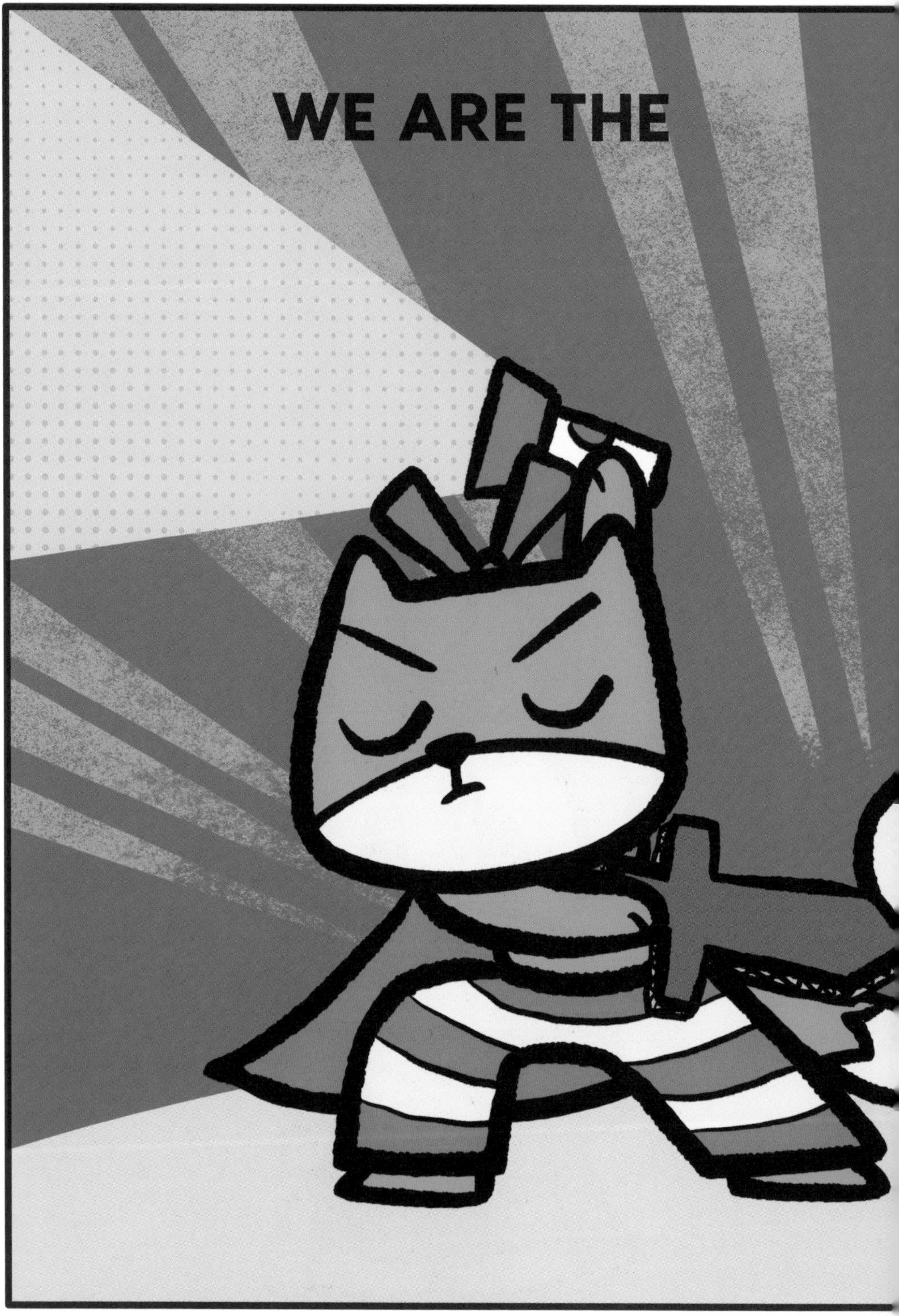
WE ARE THE

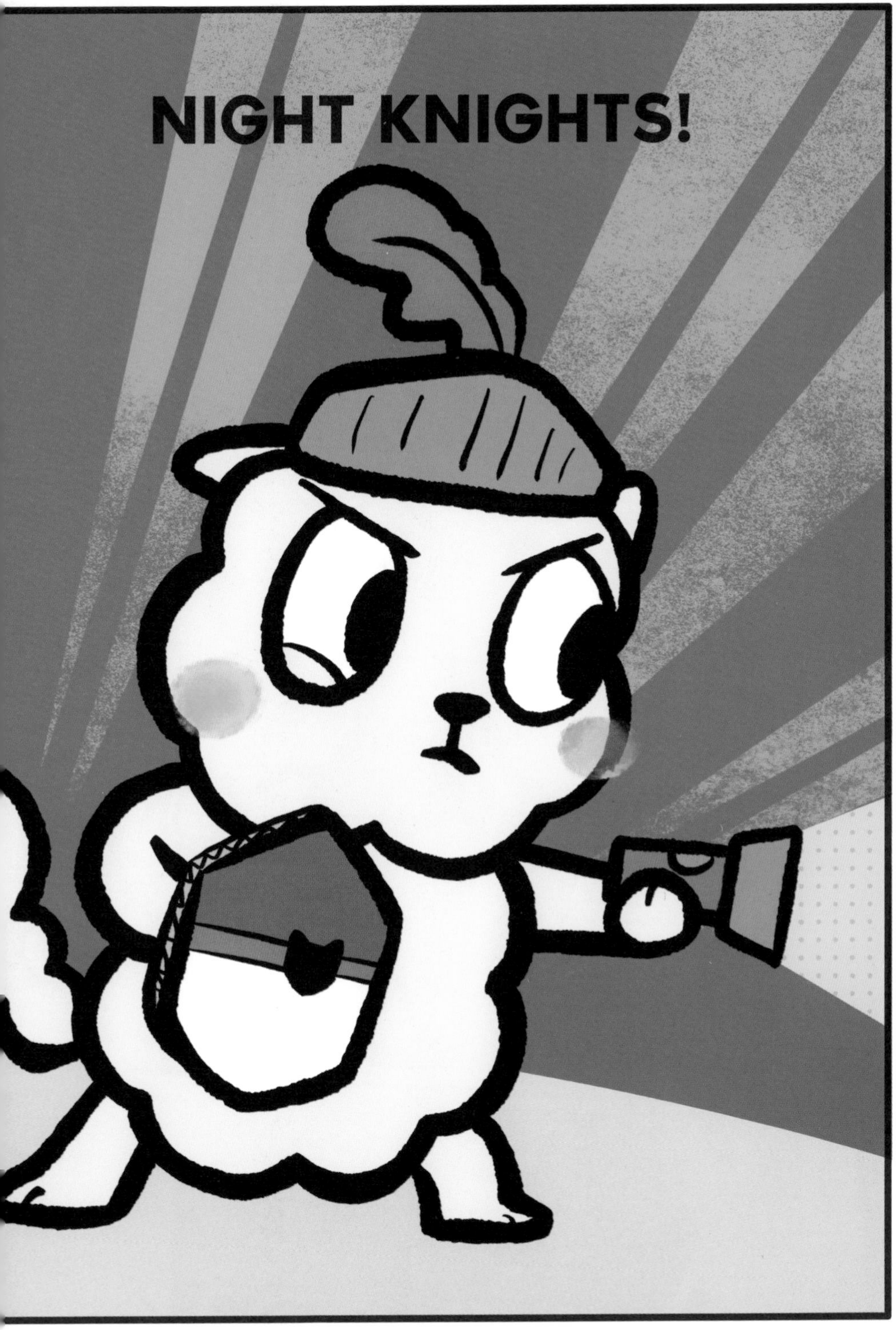
NIGHT KNIGHTS!

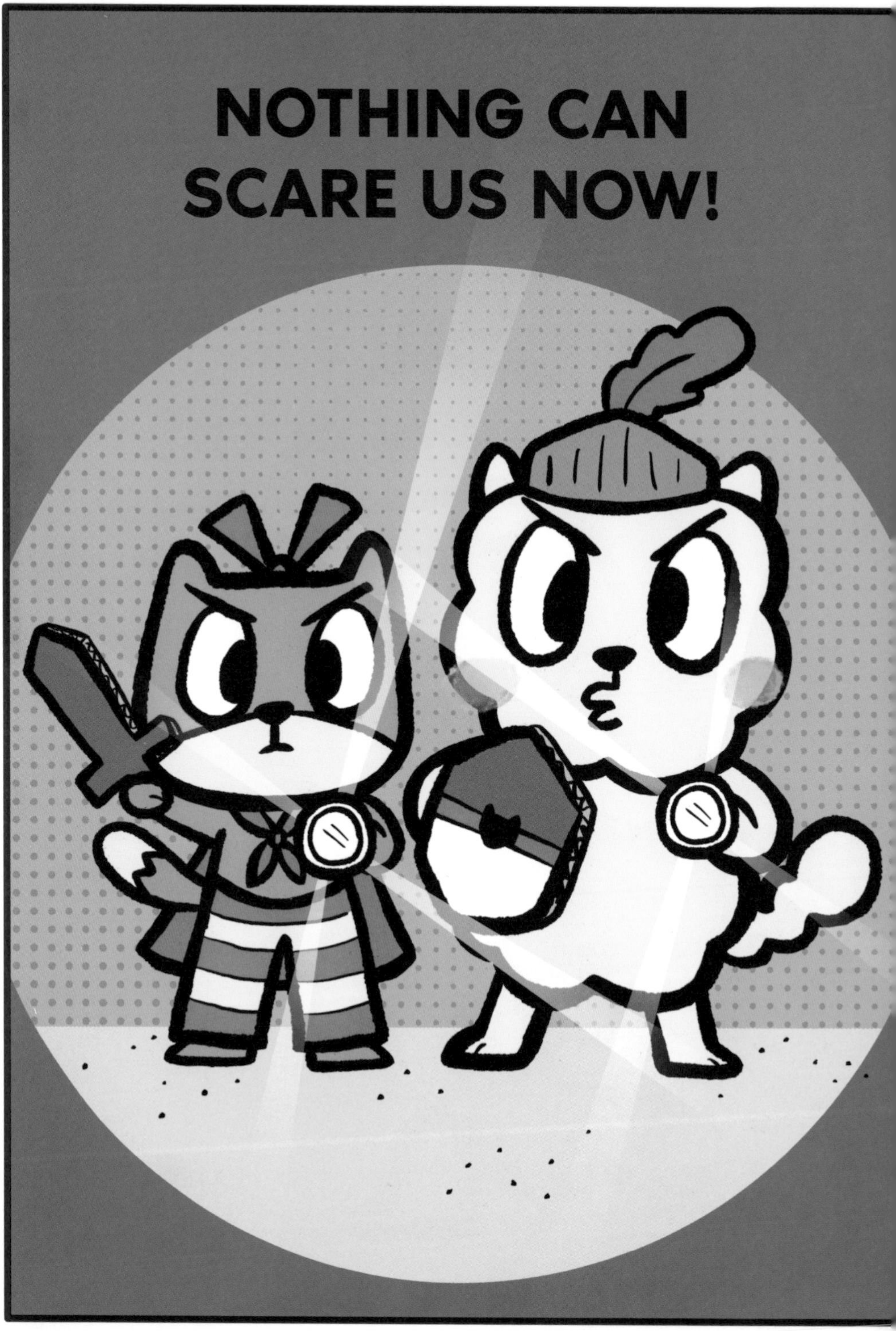
NOTHING CAN SCARE US NOW!

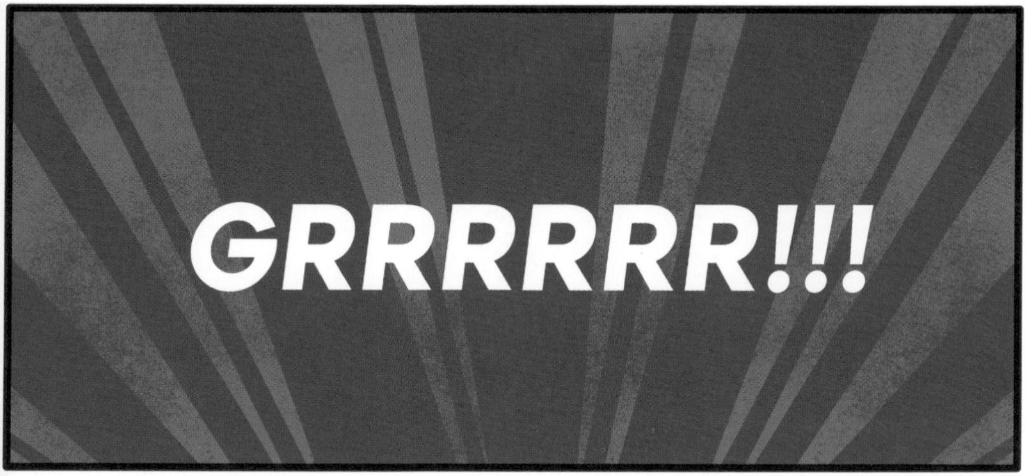
GRRRRRRR!!!

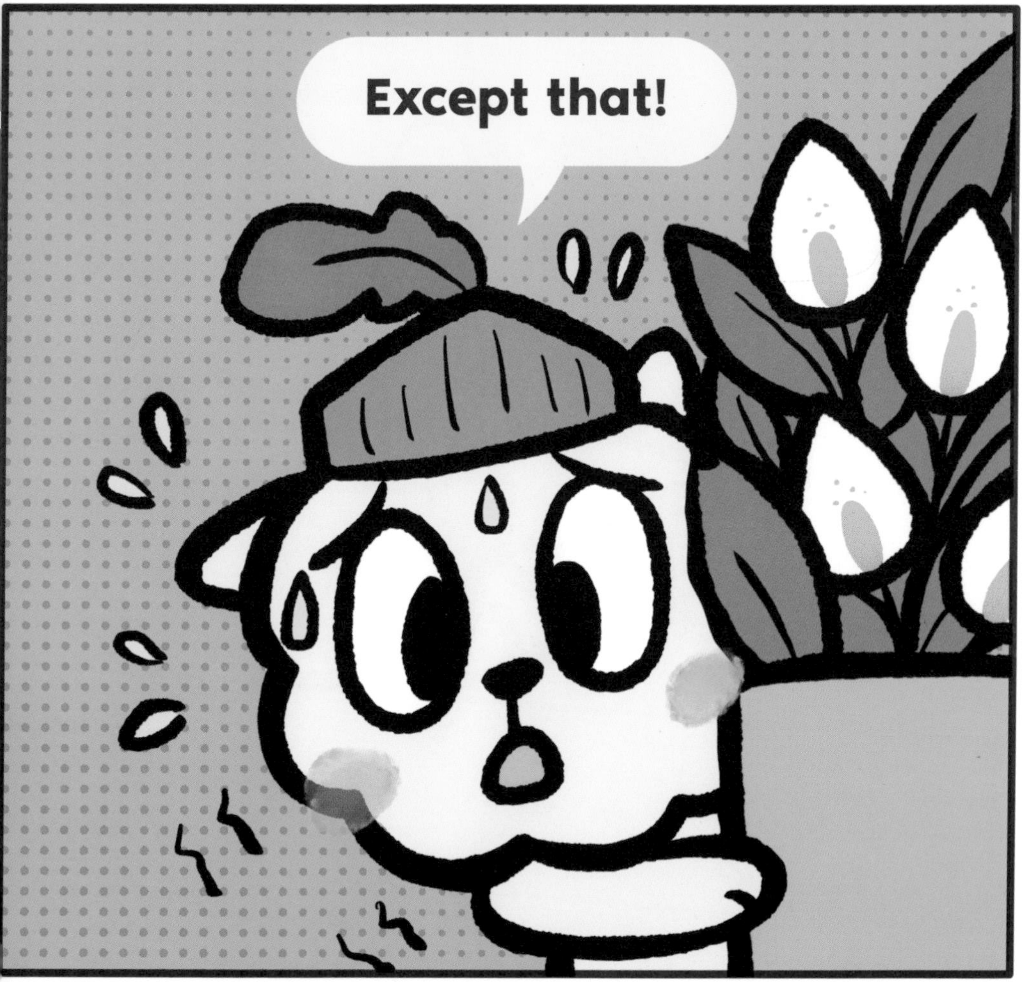
Except that!

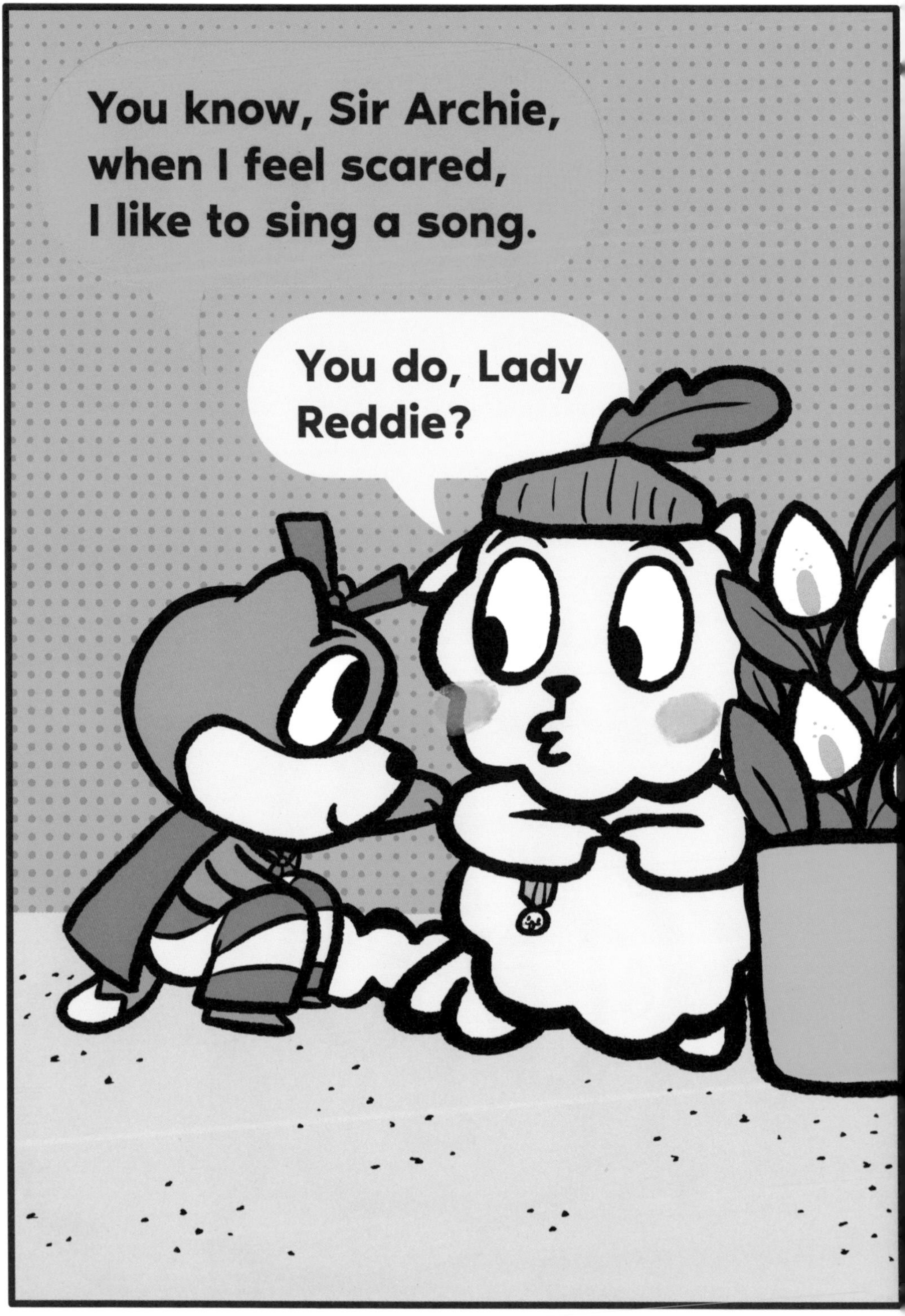
You know, Sir Archie, when I feel scared, I like to sing a song.
You do, Lady Reddie?

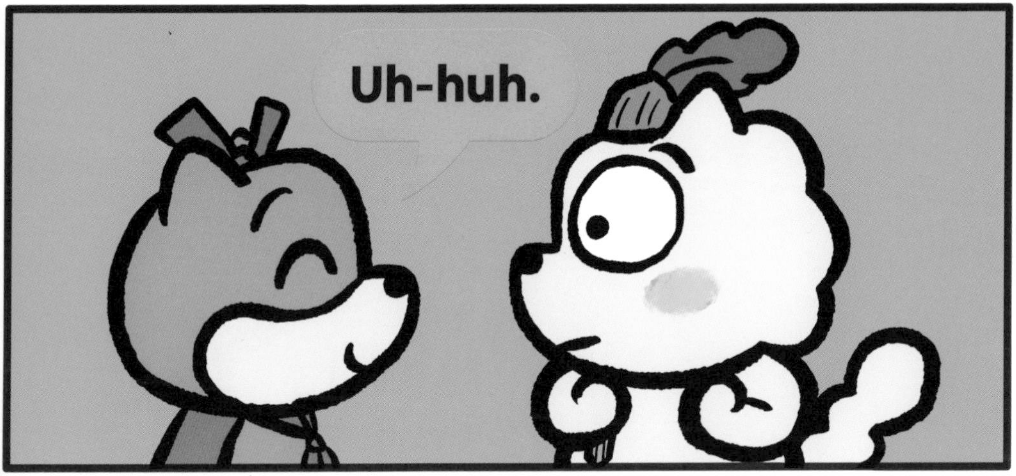
Uh-huh.

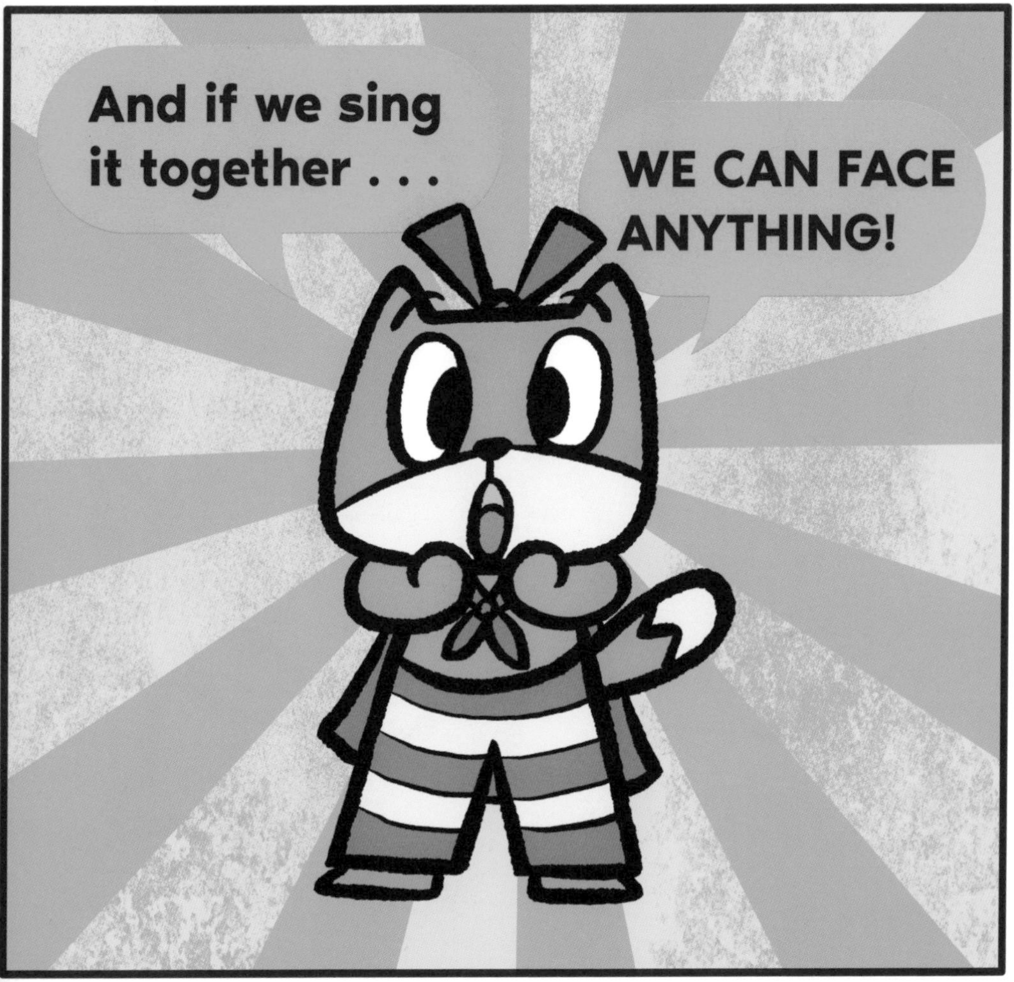
And if we sing it together . . .
WE CAN FACE ANYTHING!

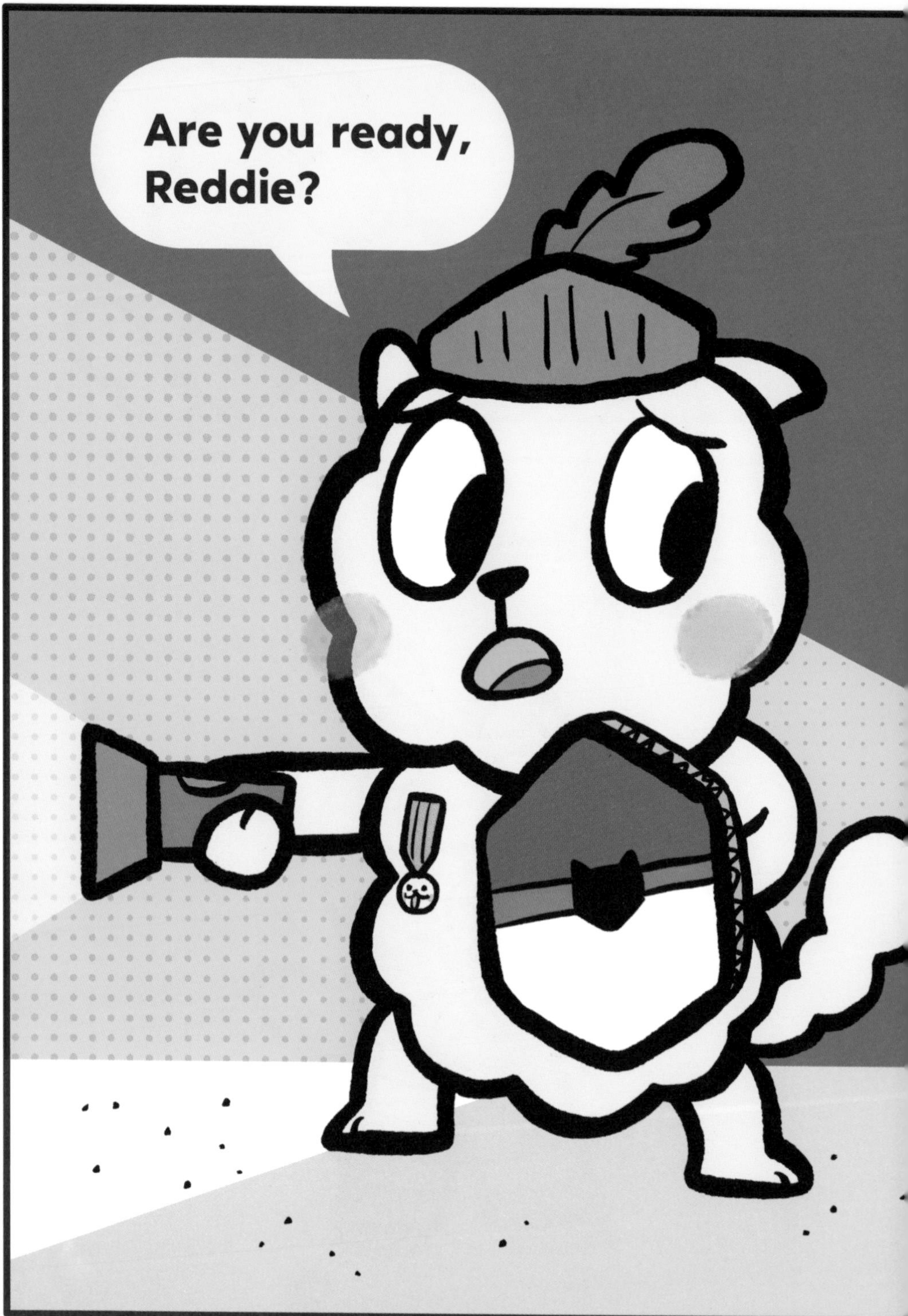
Are you ready, Reddie?

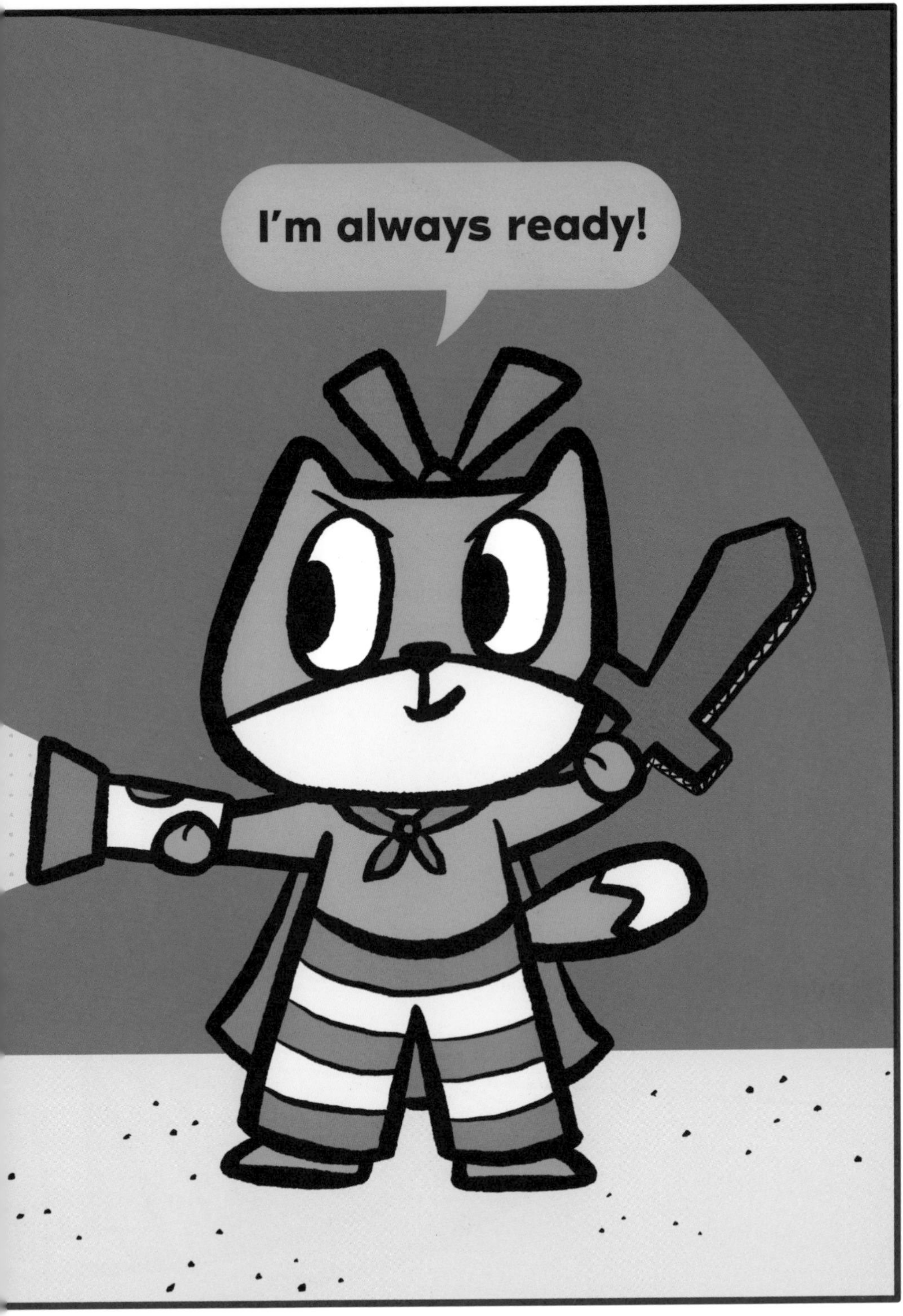
I'm always ready!

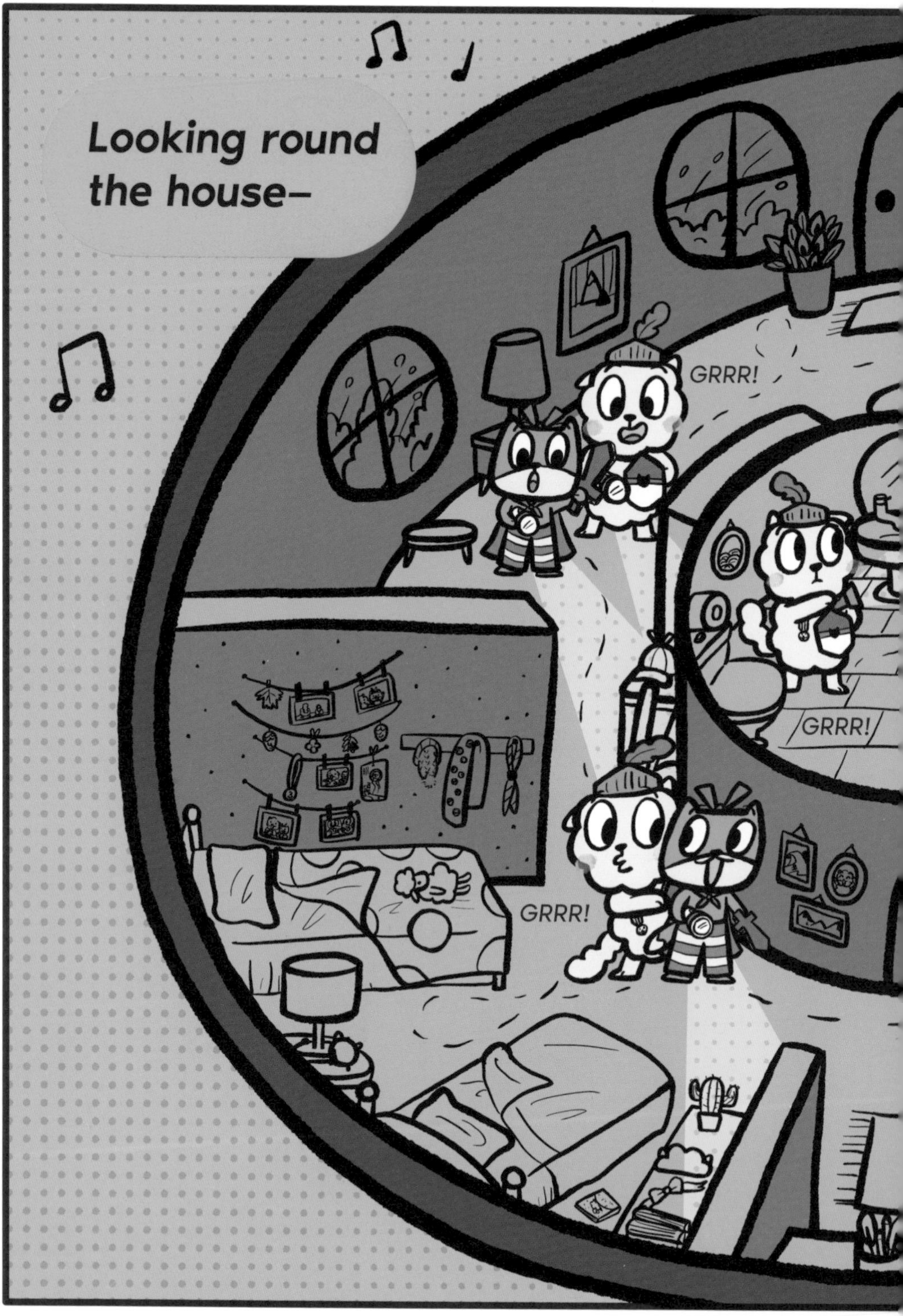
Looking round the house–
GRRR!
GRRR!
GRRR!

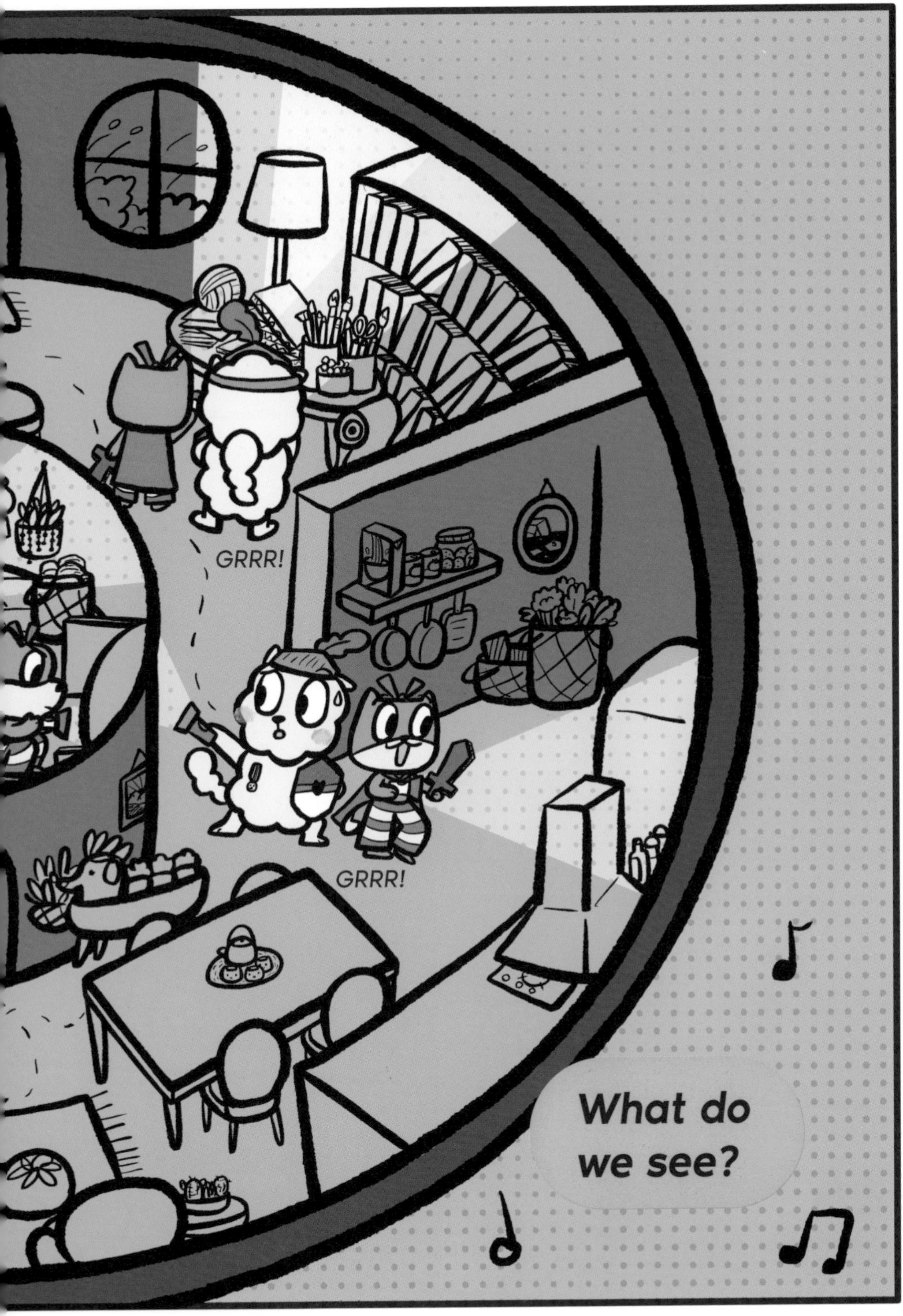
GRRR!
GRRR!
What do we see?

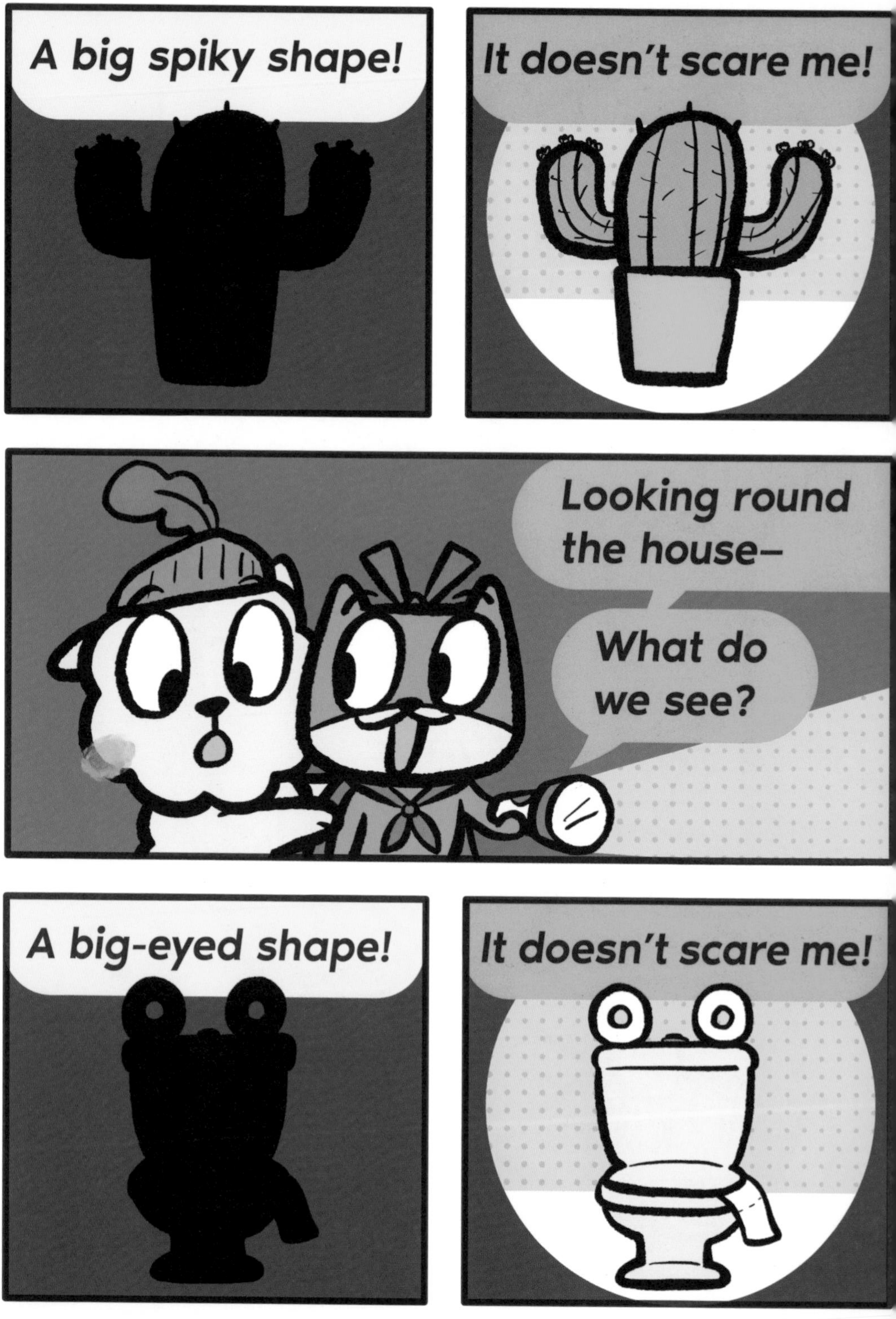
A big spiky shape!
It doesn't scare me!
Looking round the house–
What do we see?
A big-eyed shape!
It doesn't scare me!

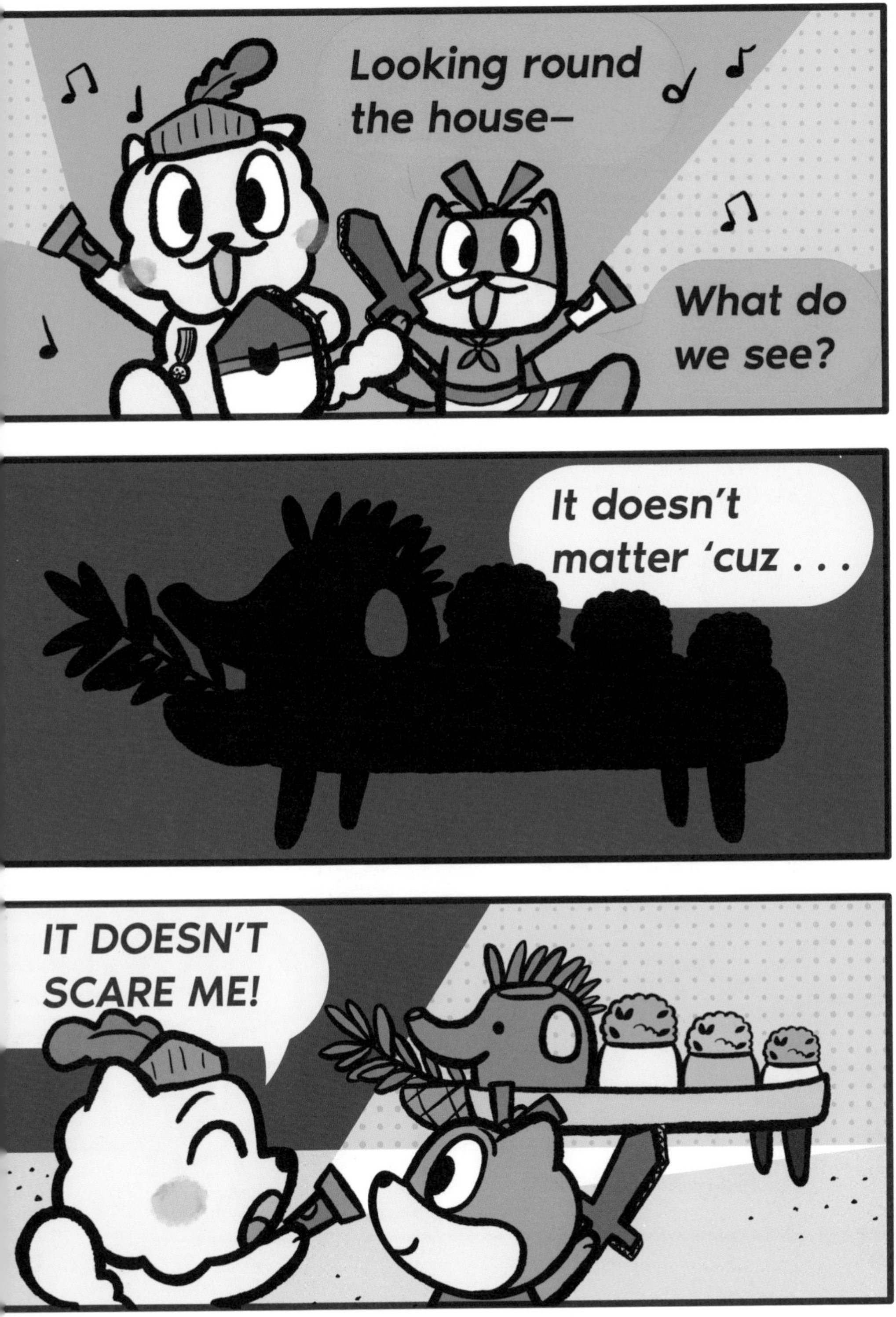
Looking round the house–
What do we see?
It doesn't matter 'cuz . . .
IT DOESN'T SCARE ME!

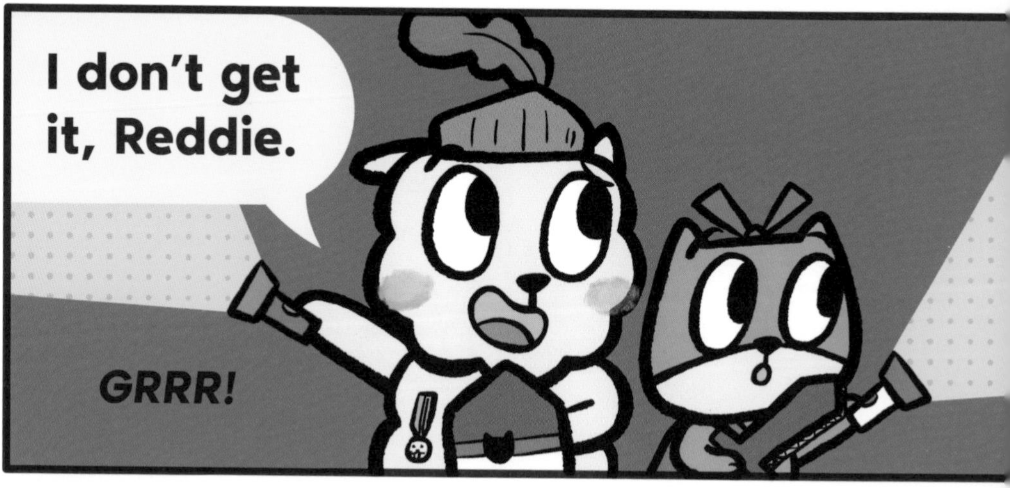
I don't get it, Reddie.
GRRR!

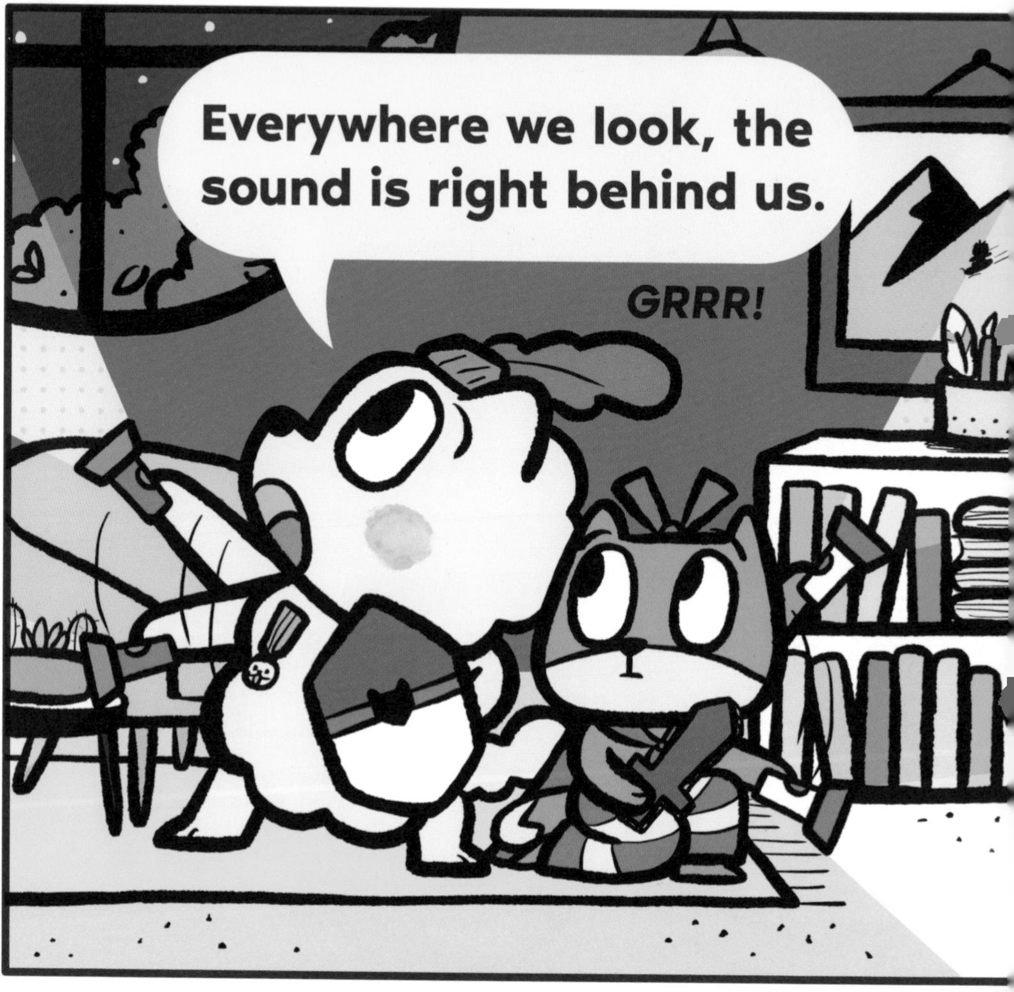
Everywhere we look, the sound is right behind us.
GRRR!

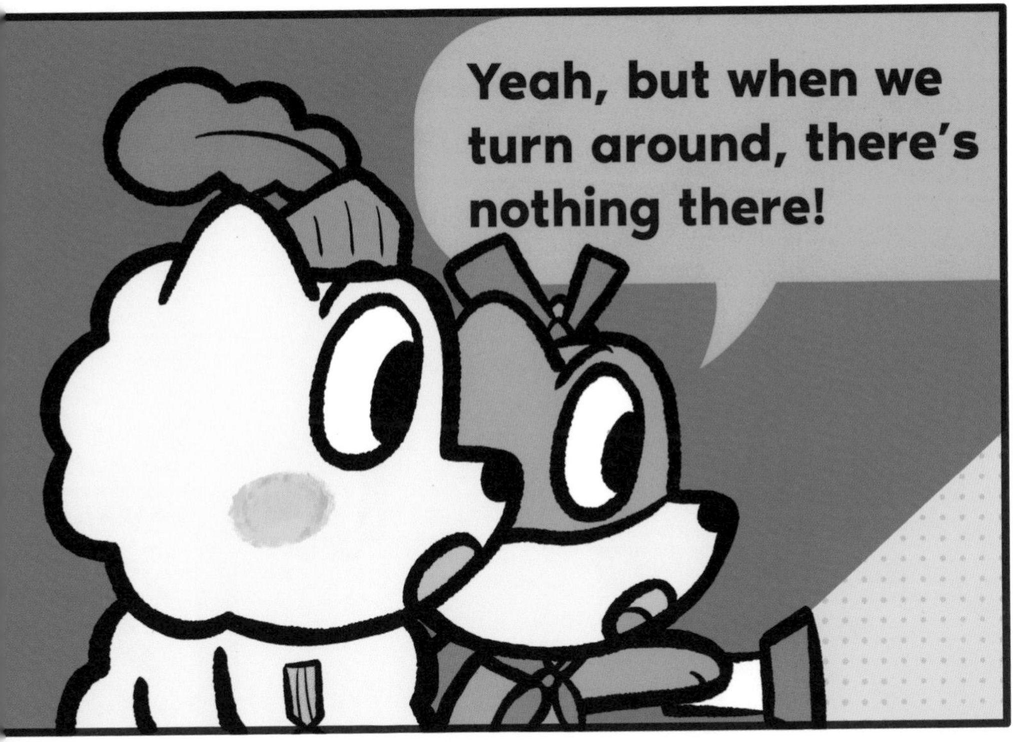
Yeah, but when we turn around, there's nothing there!

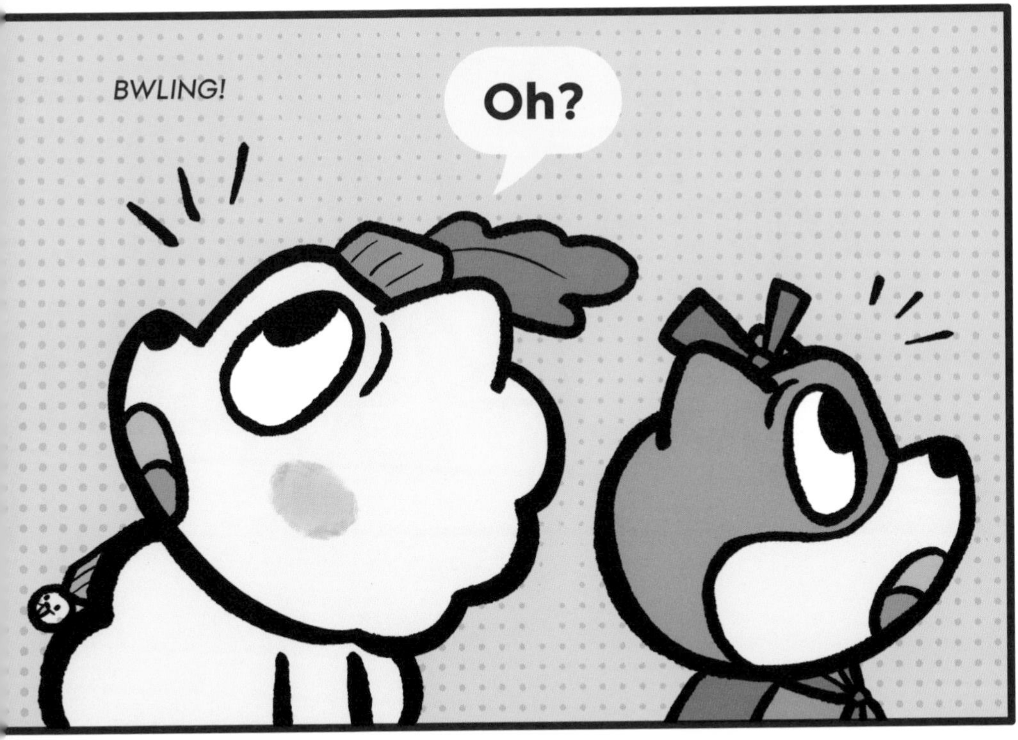
BWLING!
Oh?

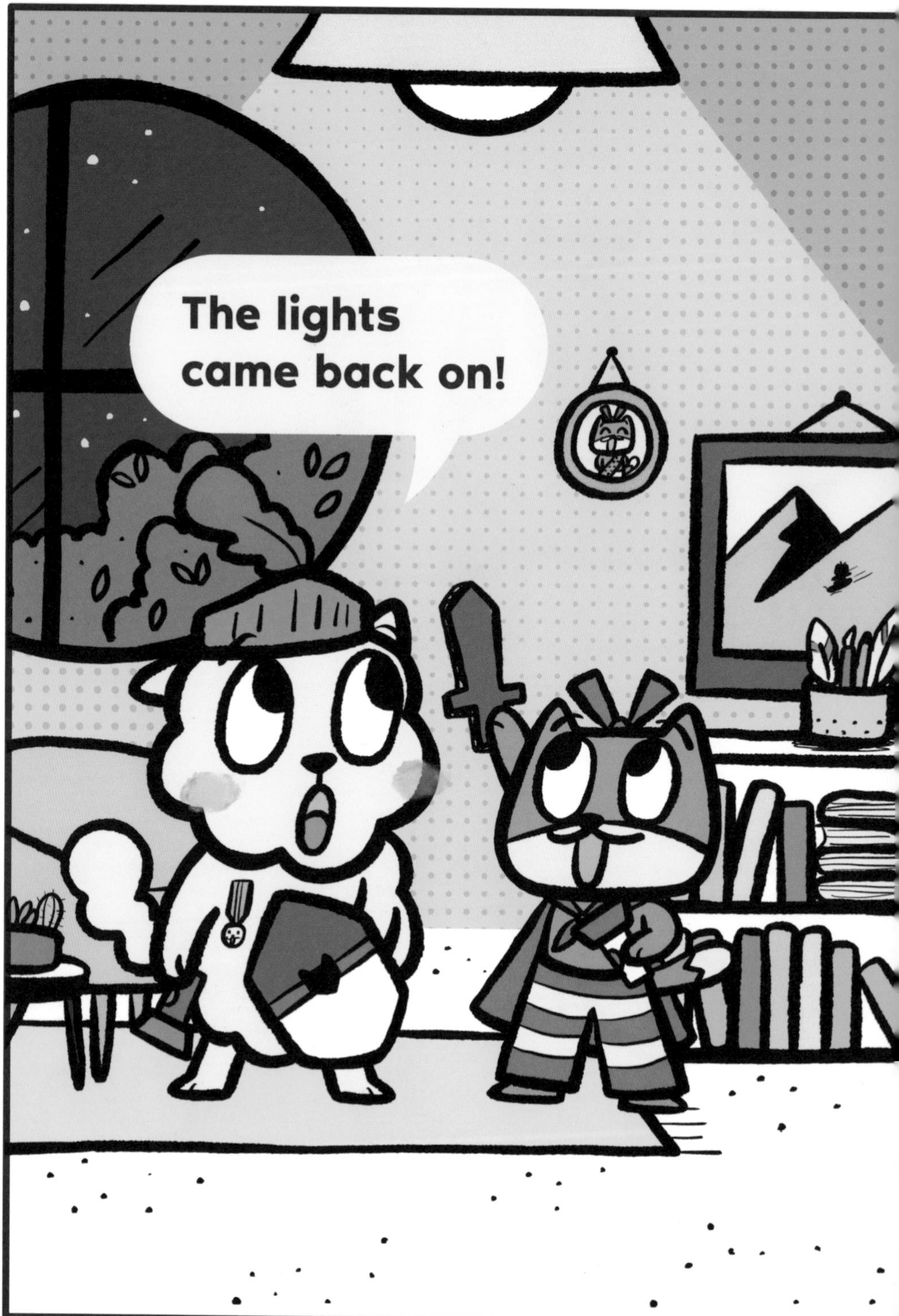
The lights came back on!

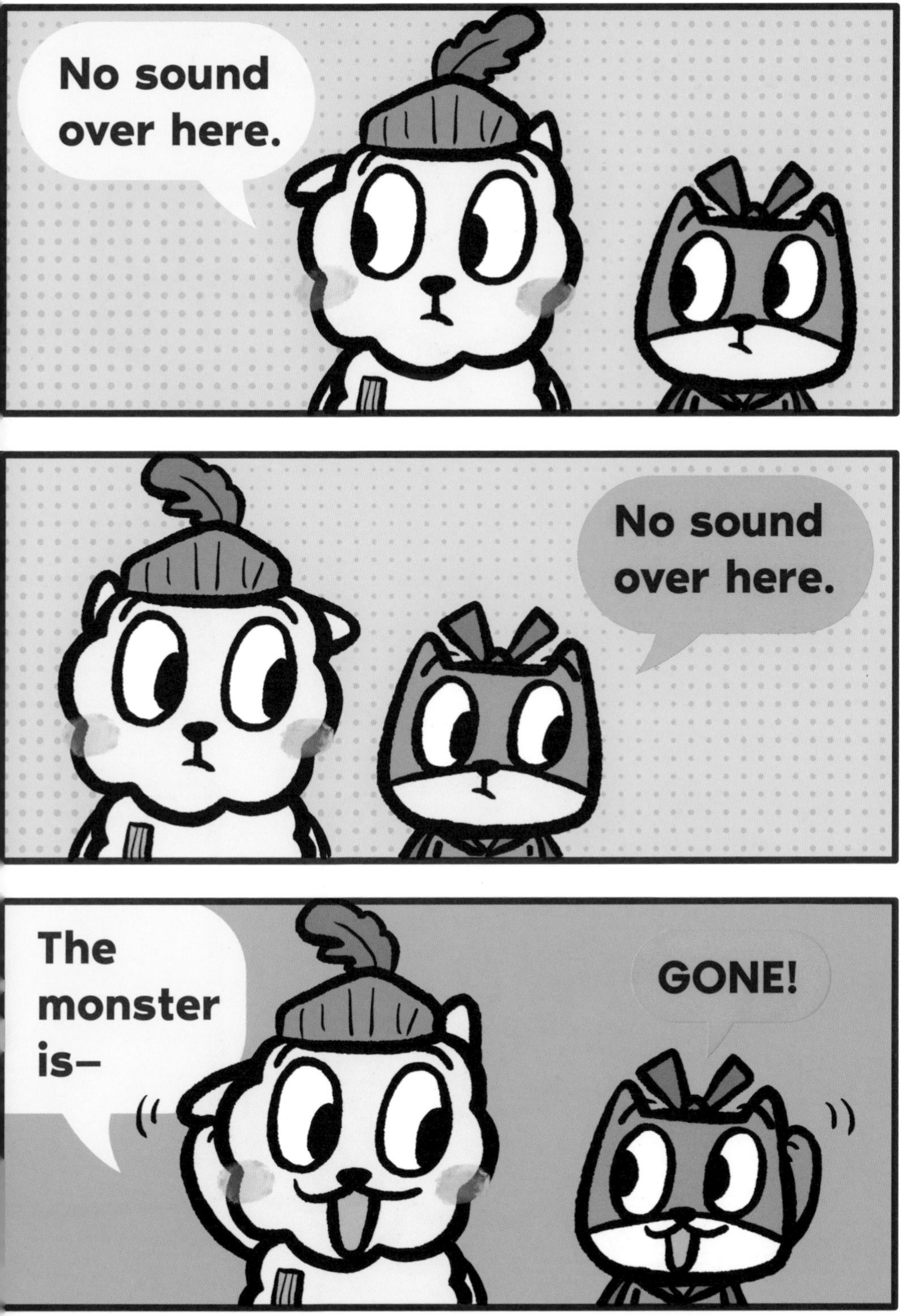
No sound over here.
No sound over here.
The monster is–
GONE!

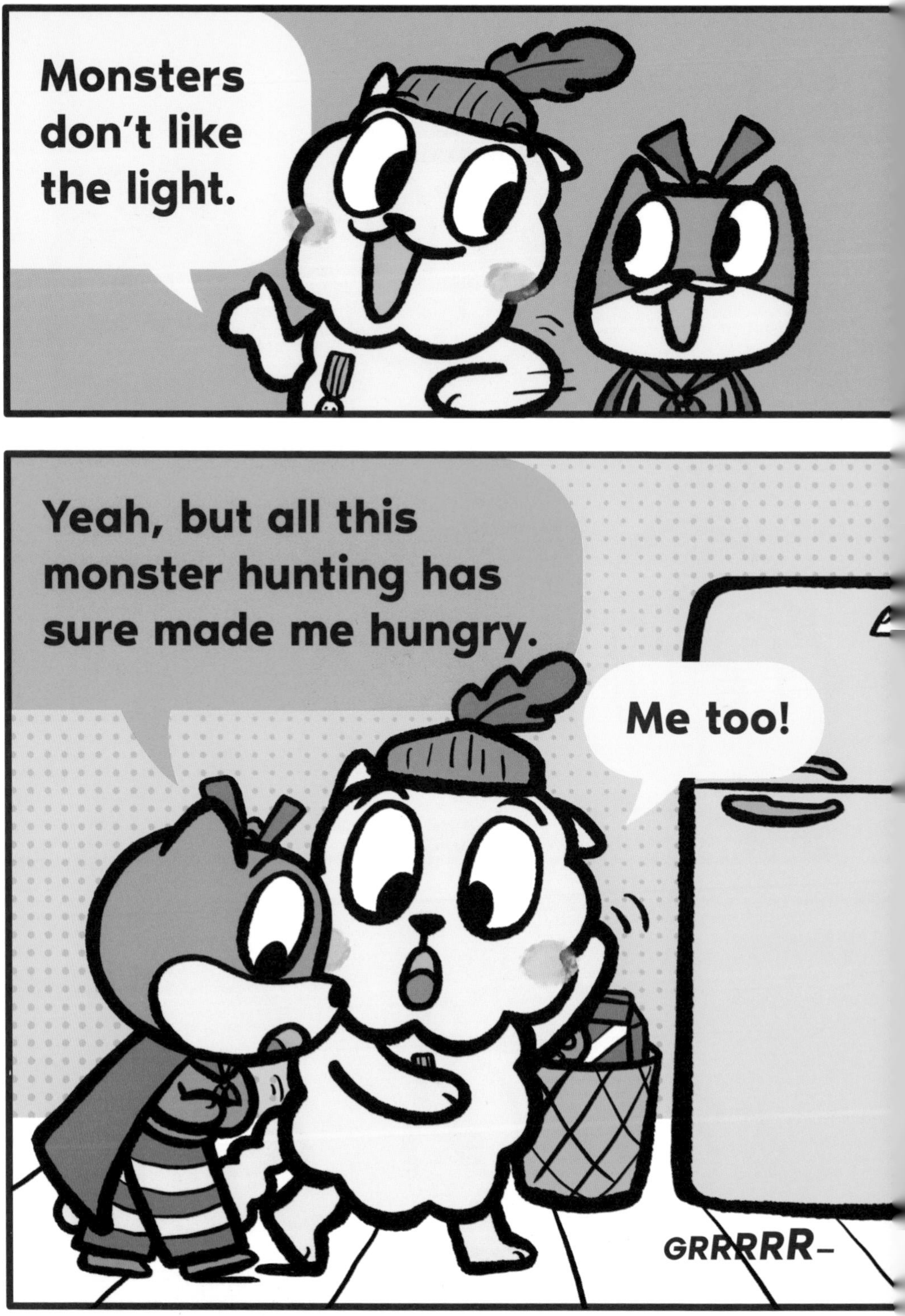
Monsters don't like the light.
Yeah, but all this monster hunting has sure made me hungry.
Me too!
GRRRRR–

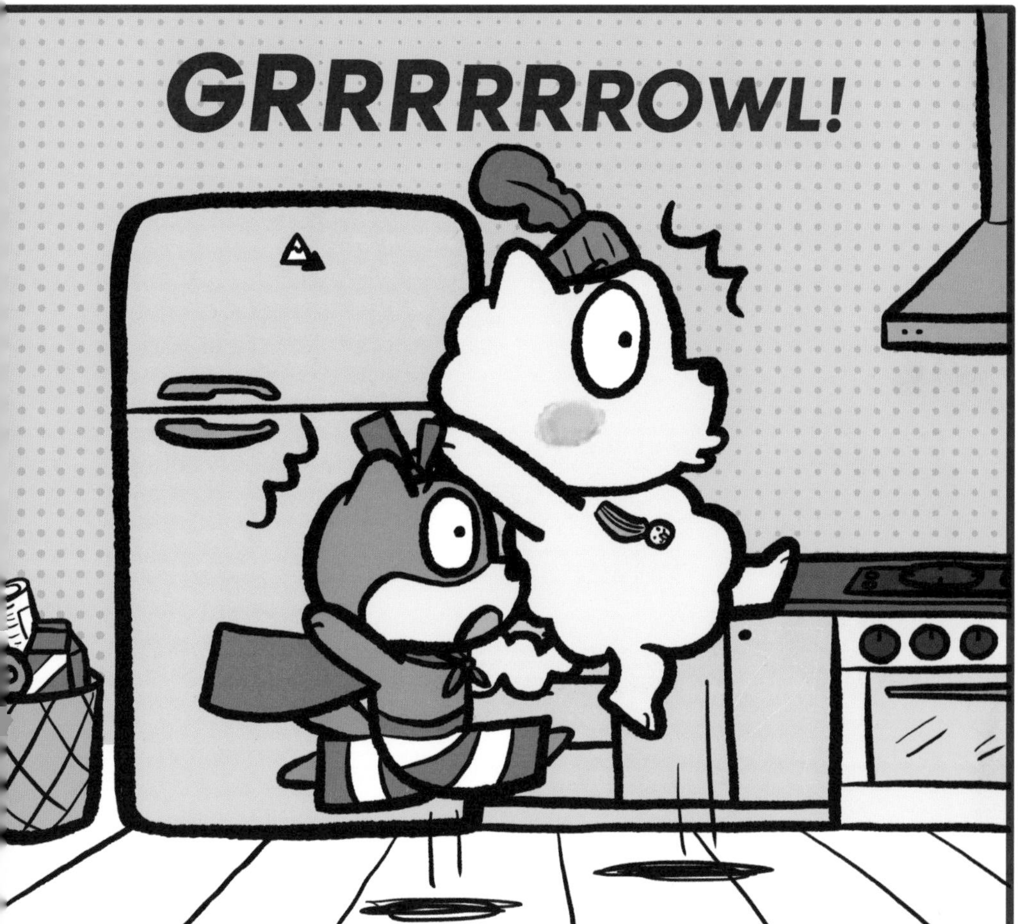
GRRRRRROWL!

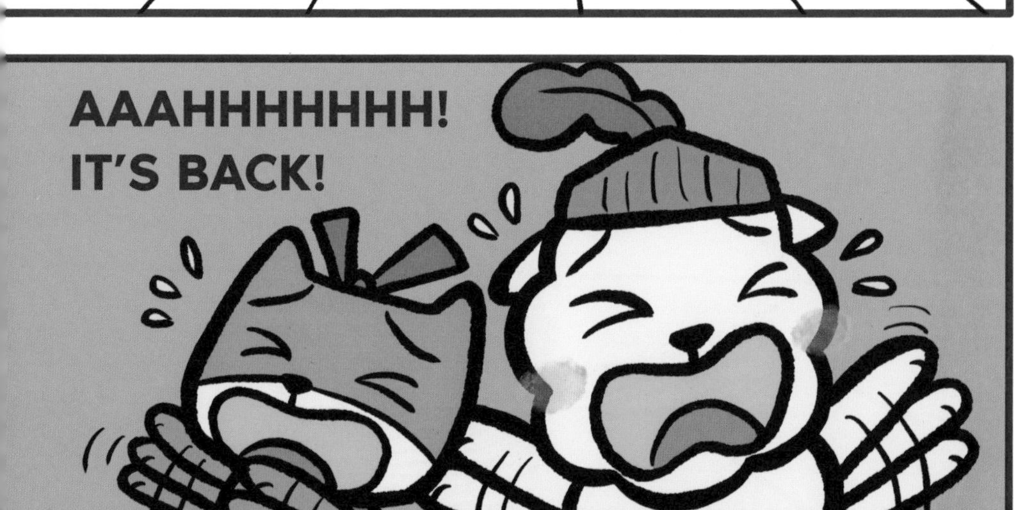
AAAHHHHHHH!
IT'S BACK!

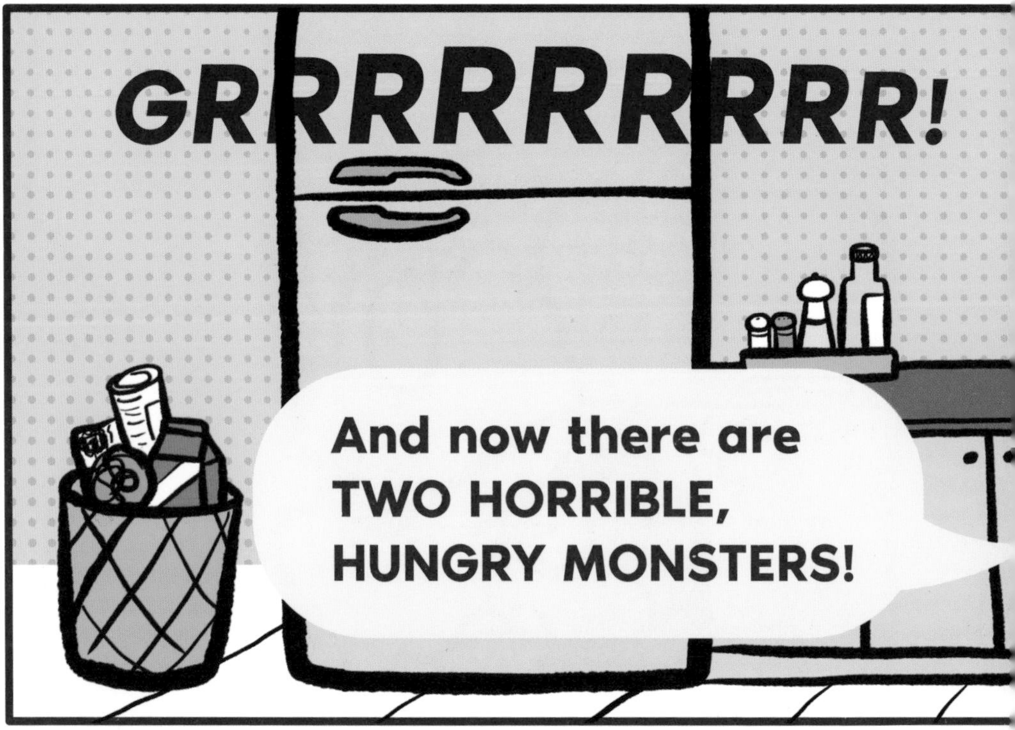
GRRRRRRRRRR!
And now there are TWO HORRIBLE, HUNGRY MONSTERS!

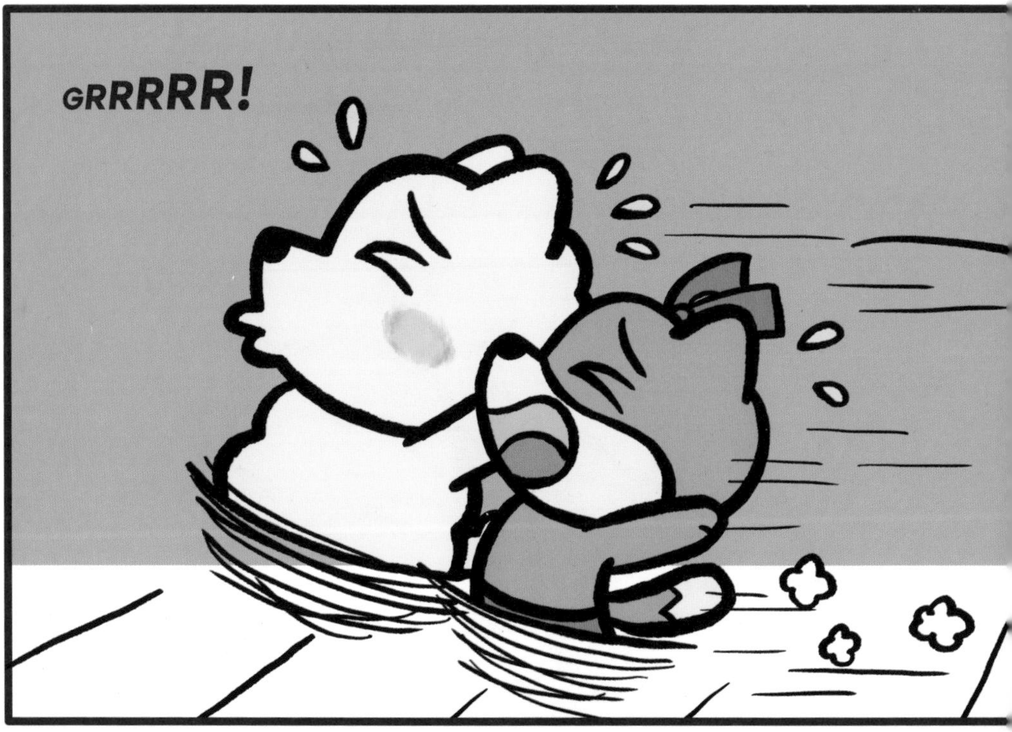
GRRRRR!

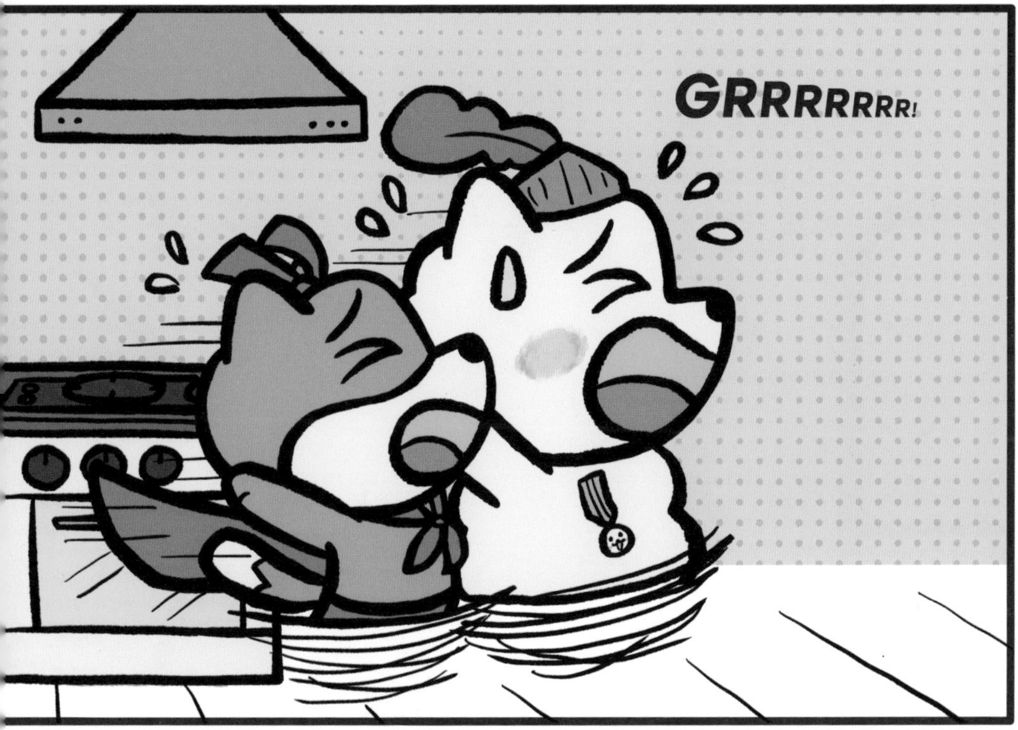
GRRRRRRR!

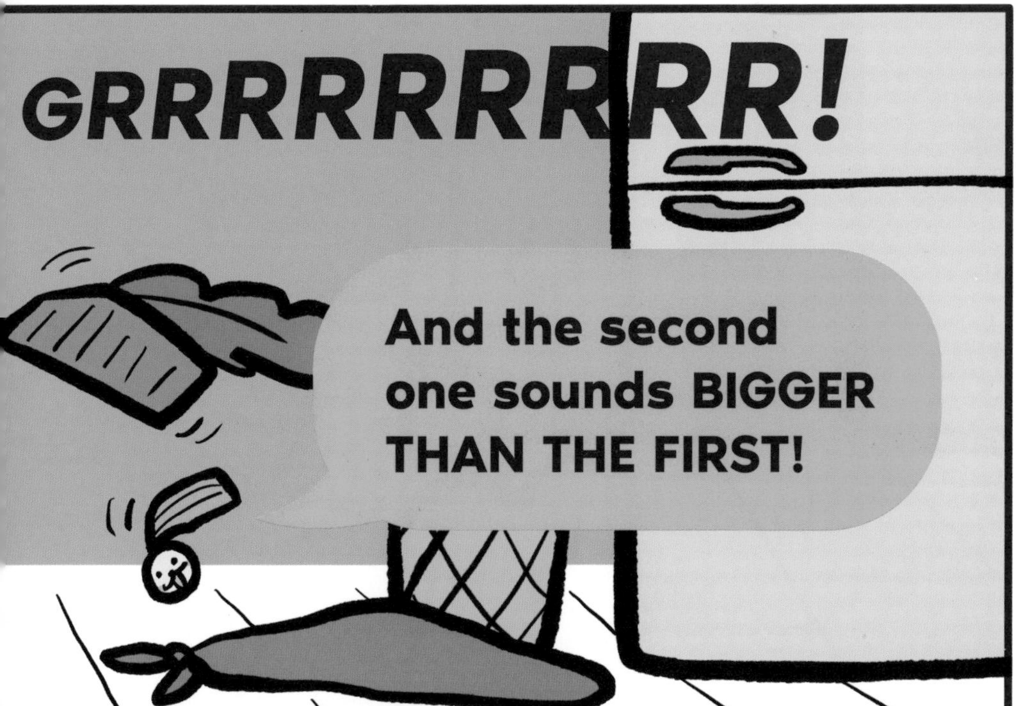
GRRRRRRRRRR!
And the second one sounds BIGGER THAN THE FIRST!

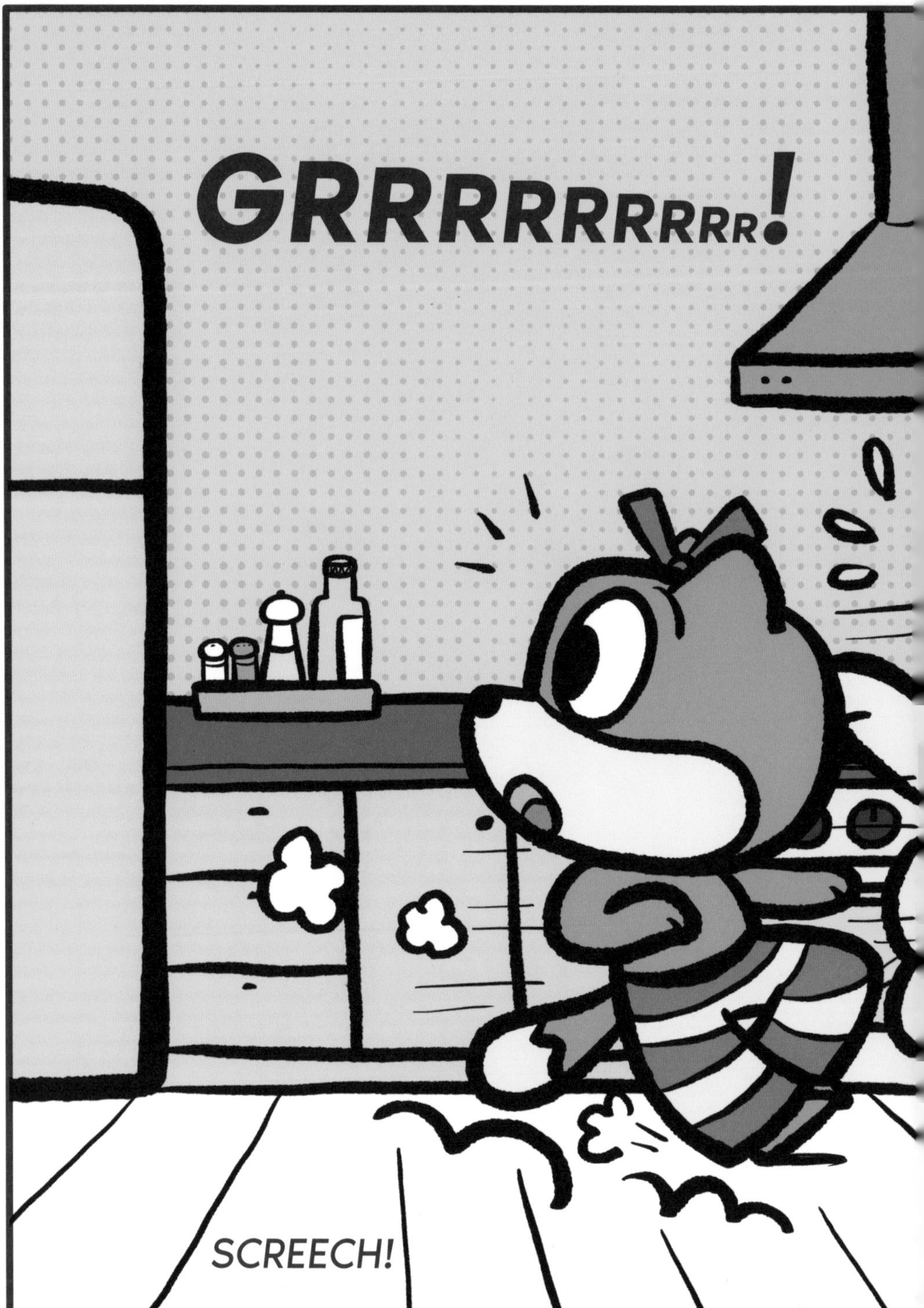
GRRRRRRRRR!
SCREECH!

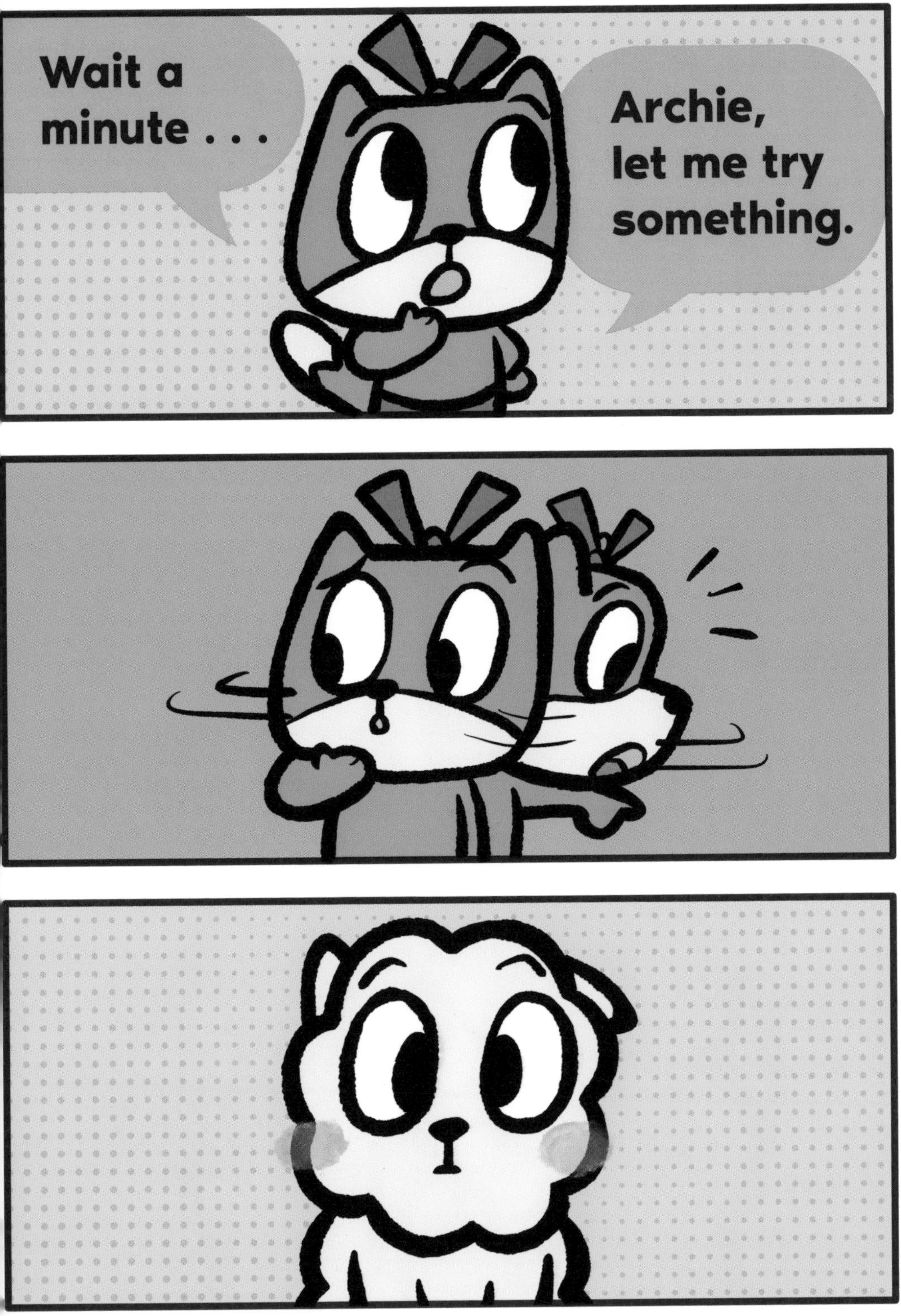
Wait a minute . . .
Archie, let me try something.

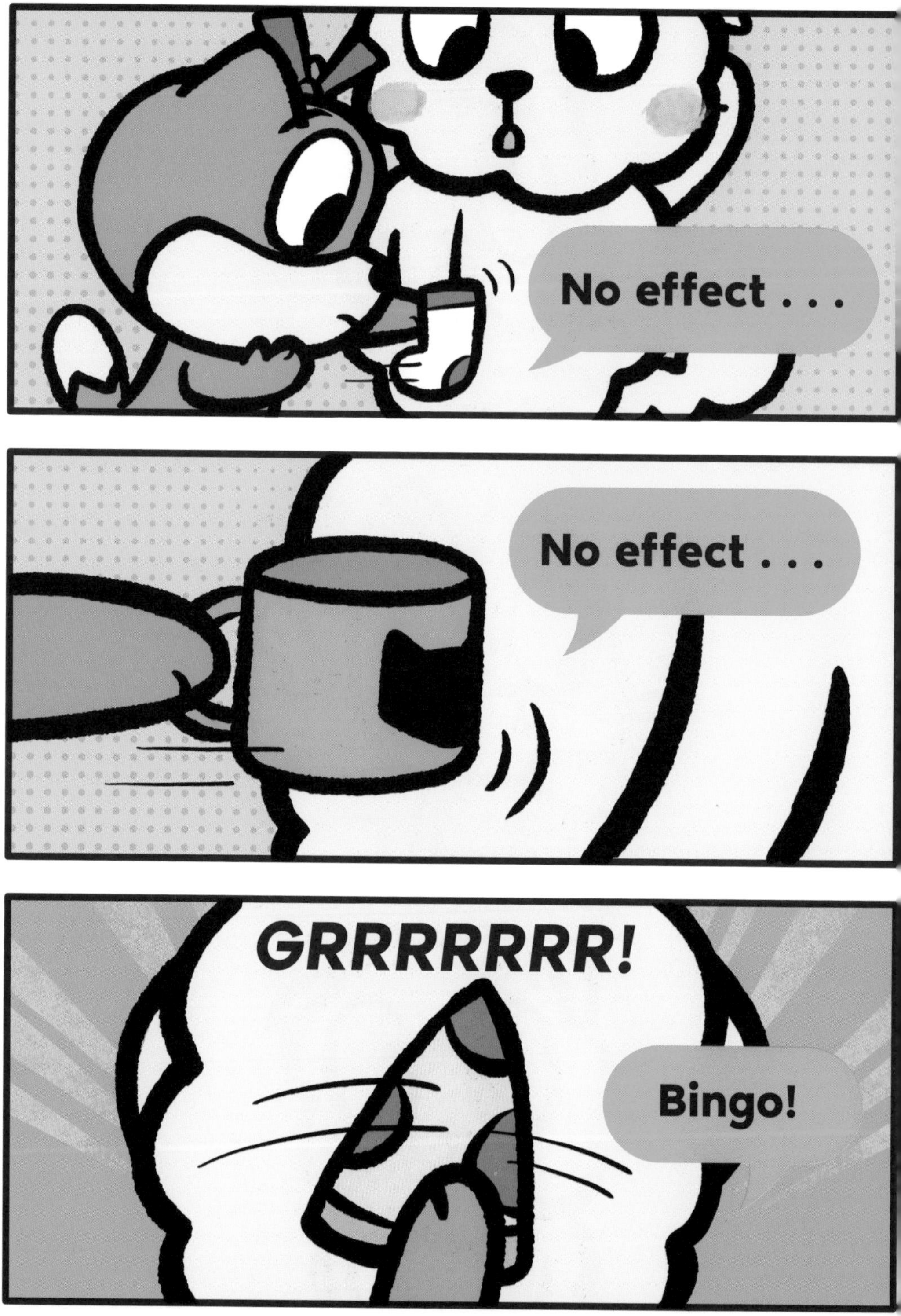
No effect . . .
No effect . . .
GRRRRRRR!
Bingo!

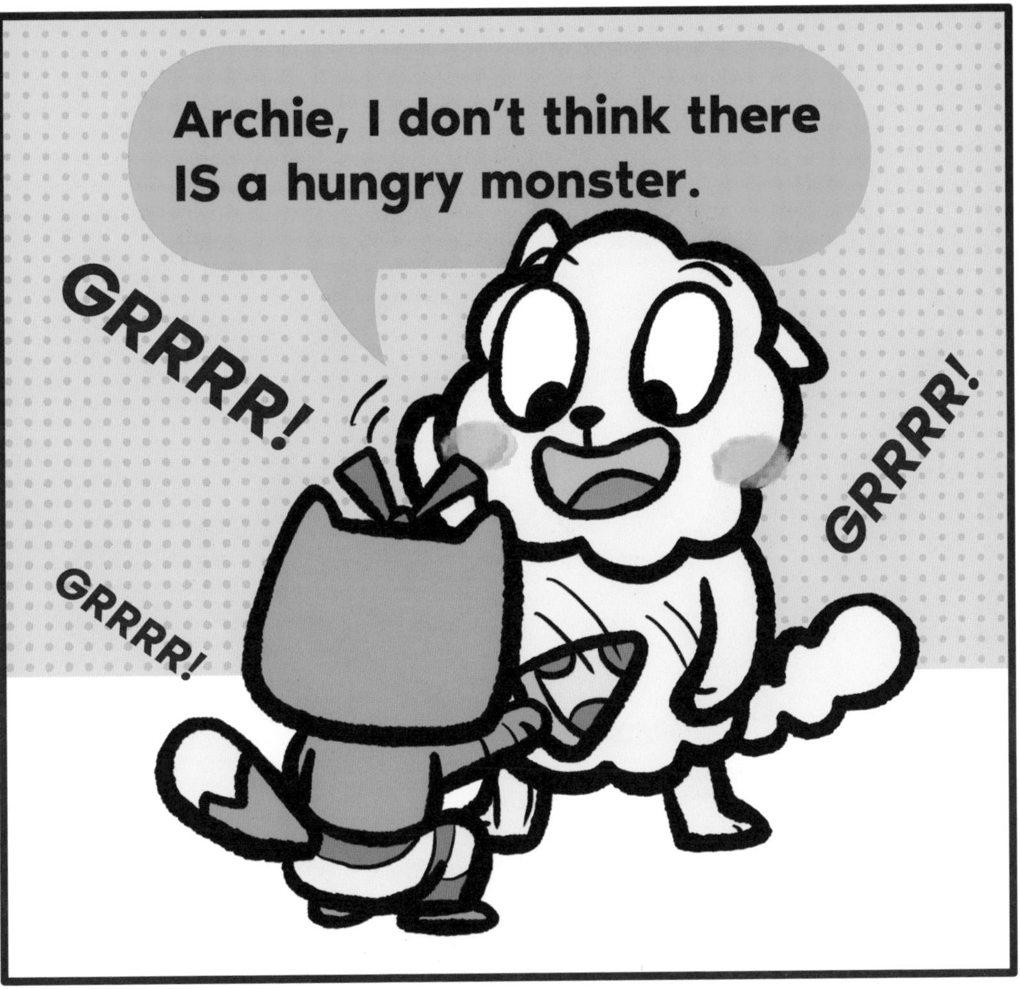
Archie, I don't think there IS a hungry monster.
GRRRRR!
GRRRR!
GRRRRR!

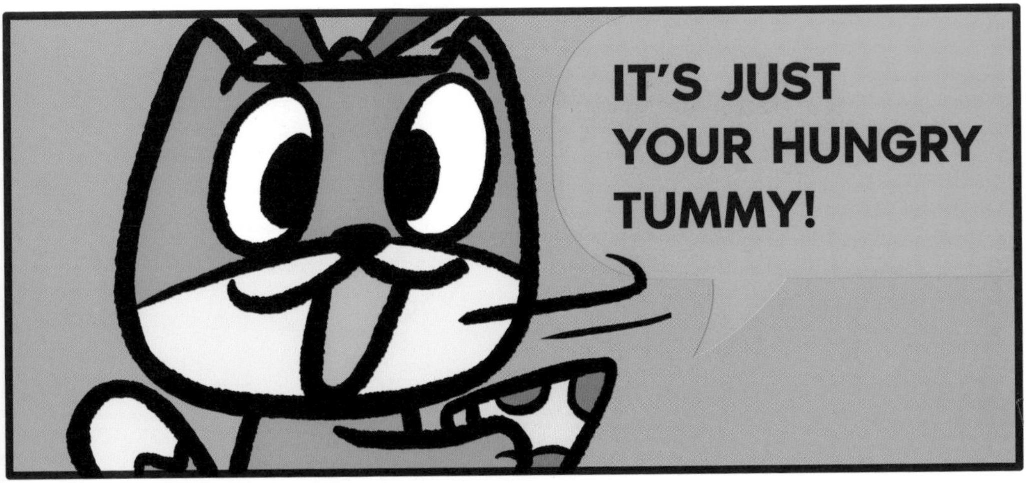
IT'S JUST YOUR HUNGRY TUMMY!

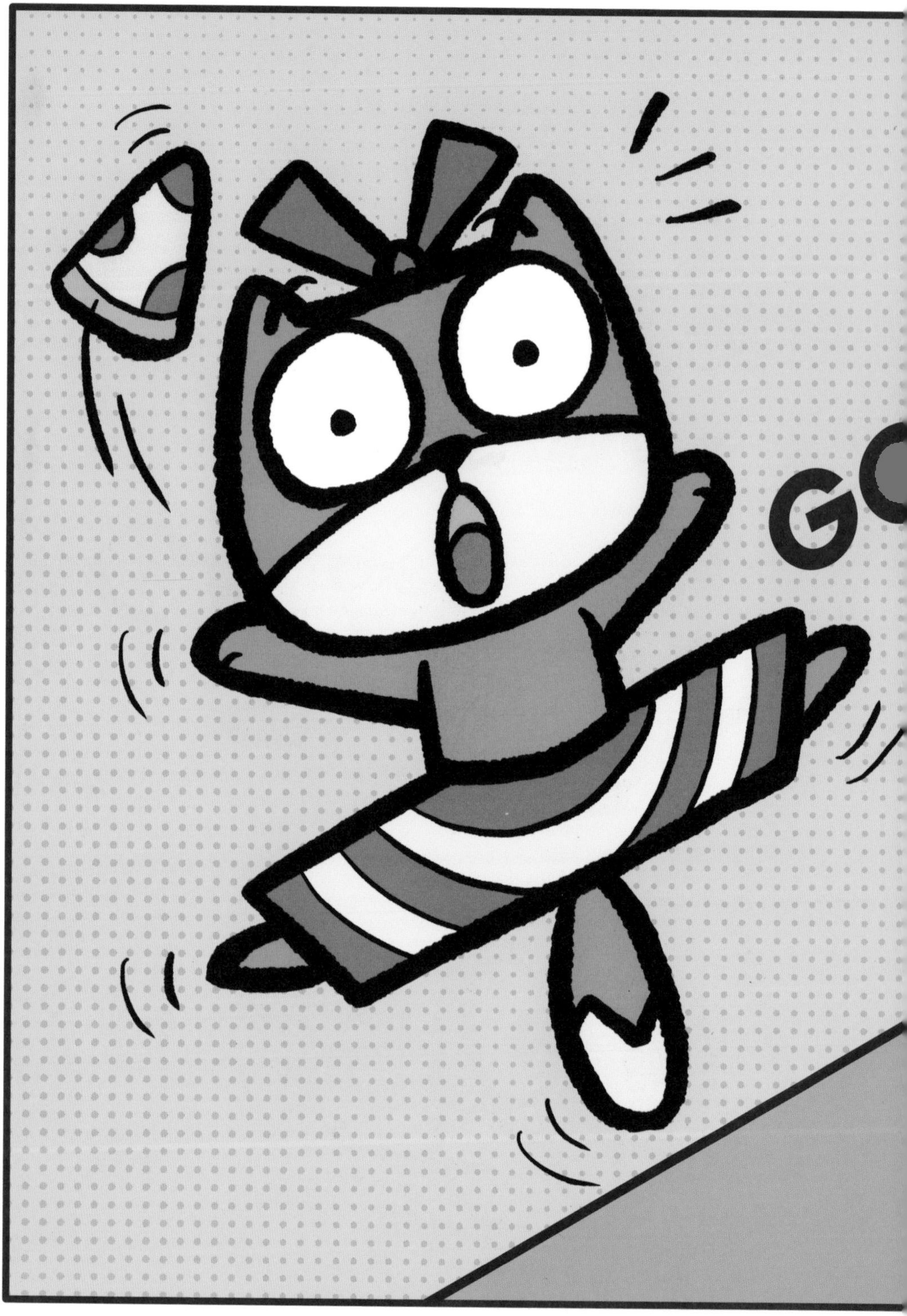

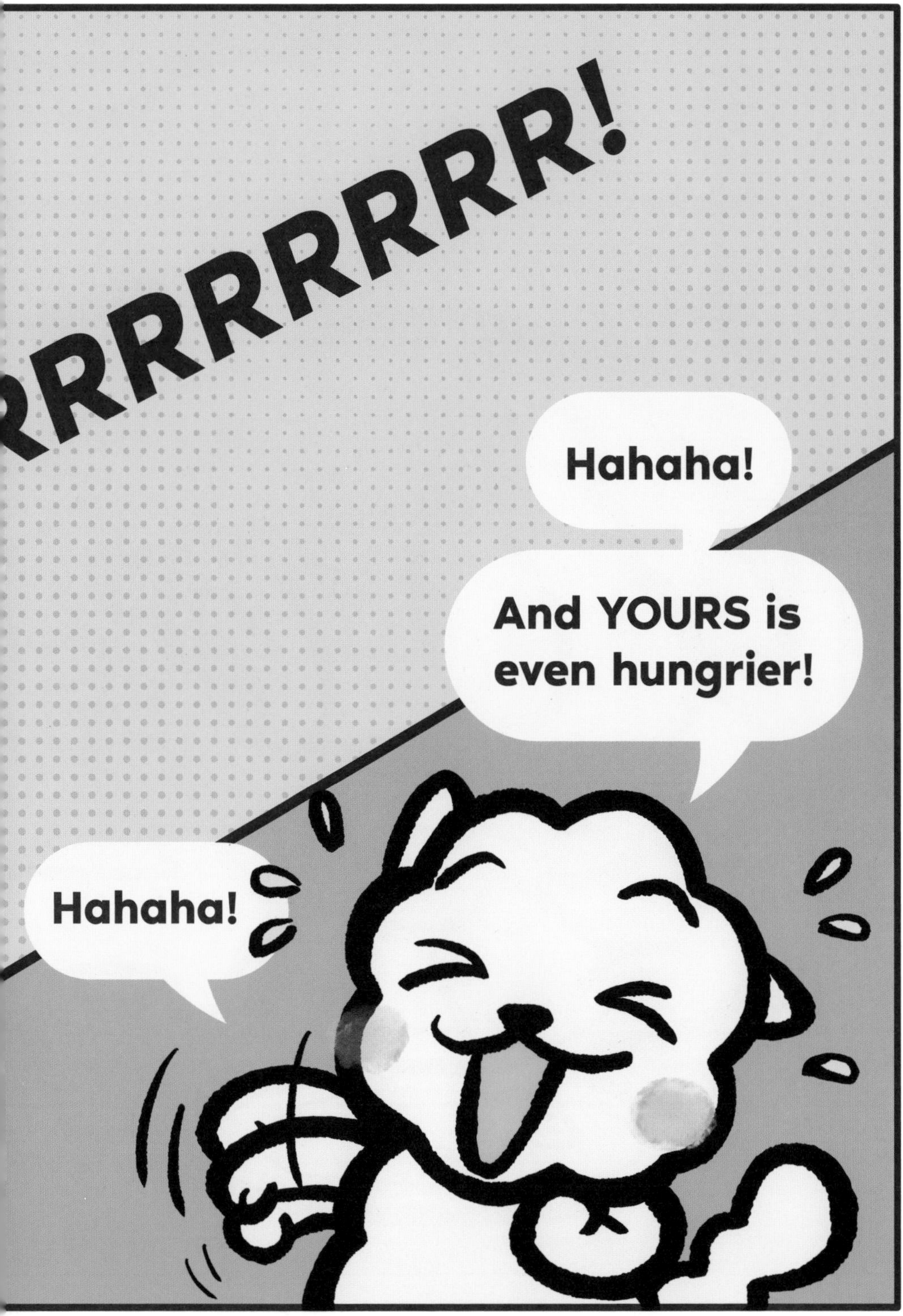
RRRRRRRRRR!
Hahaha!
And YOURS is even hungrier!
Hahaha!

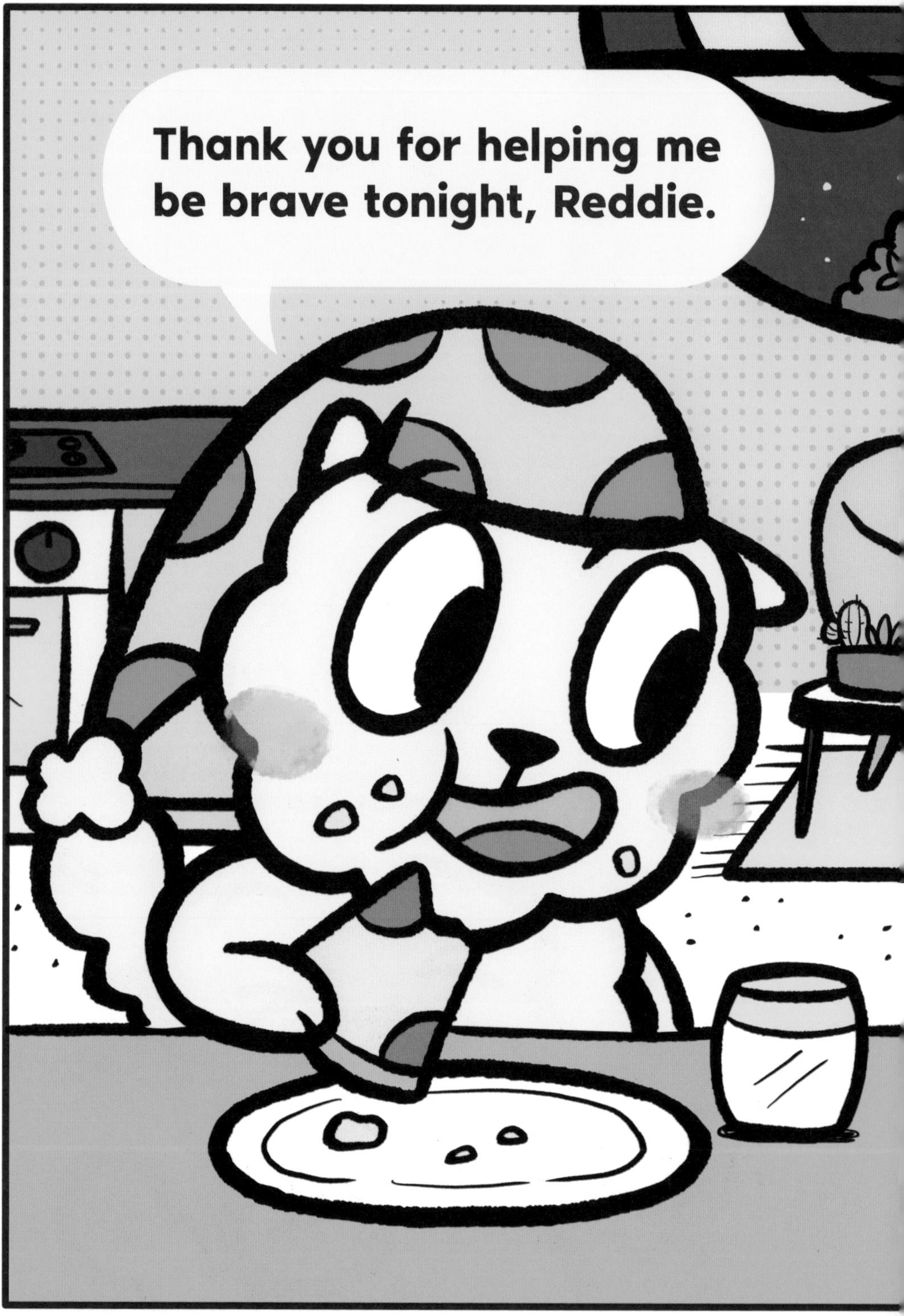
Thank you for helping me be brave tonight, Reddie.

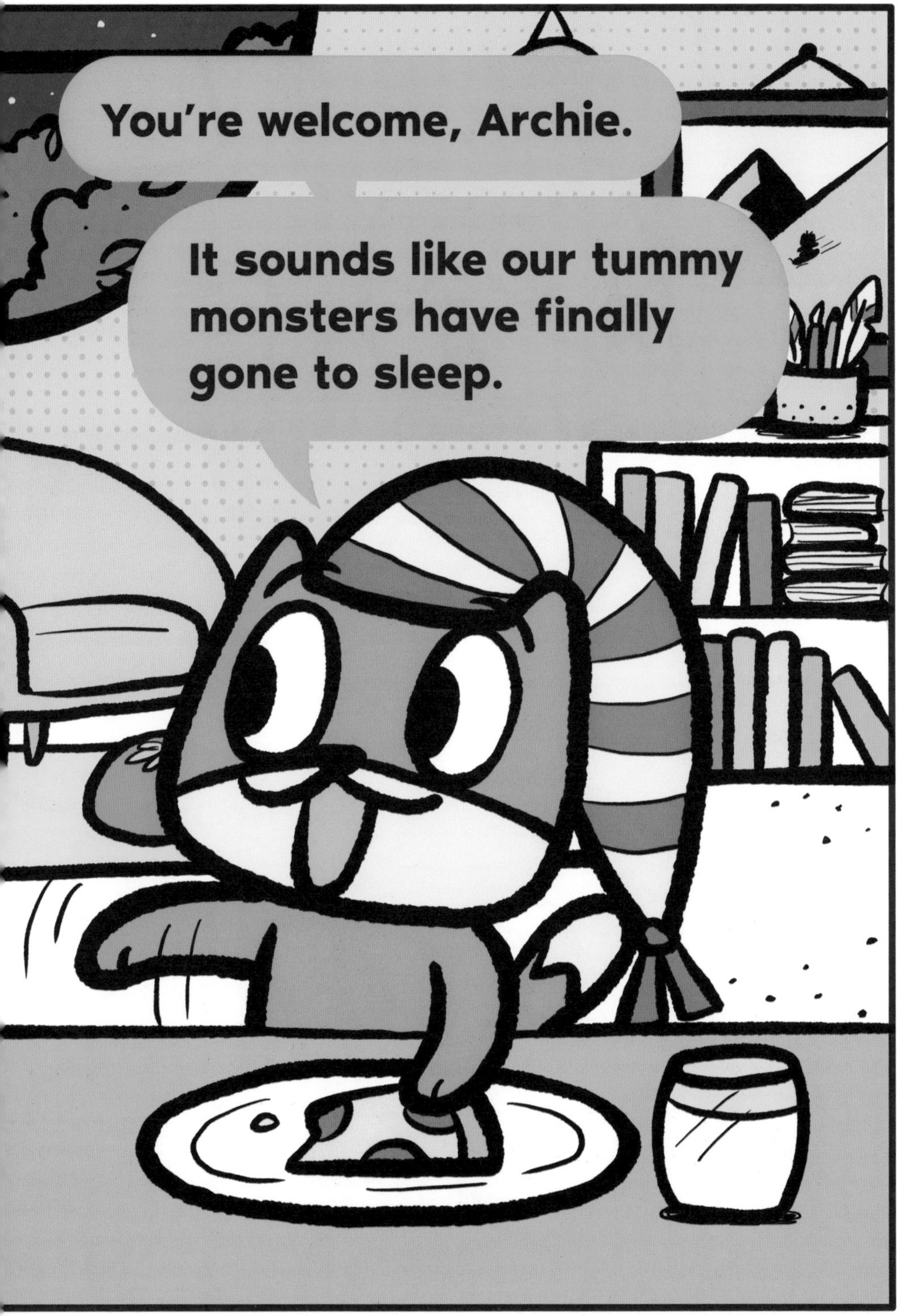
You're welcome, Archie.
It sounds like our tummy monsters have finally gone to sleep.

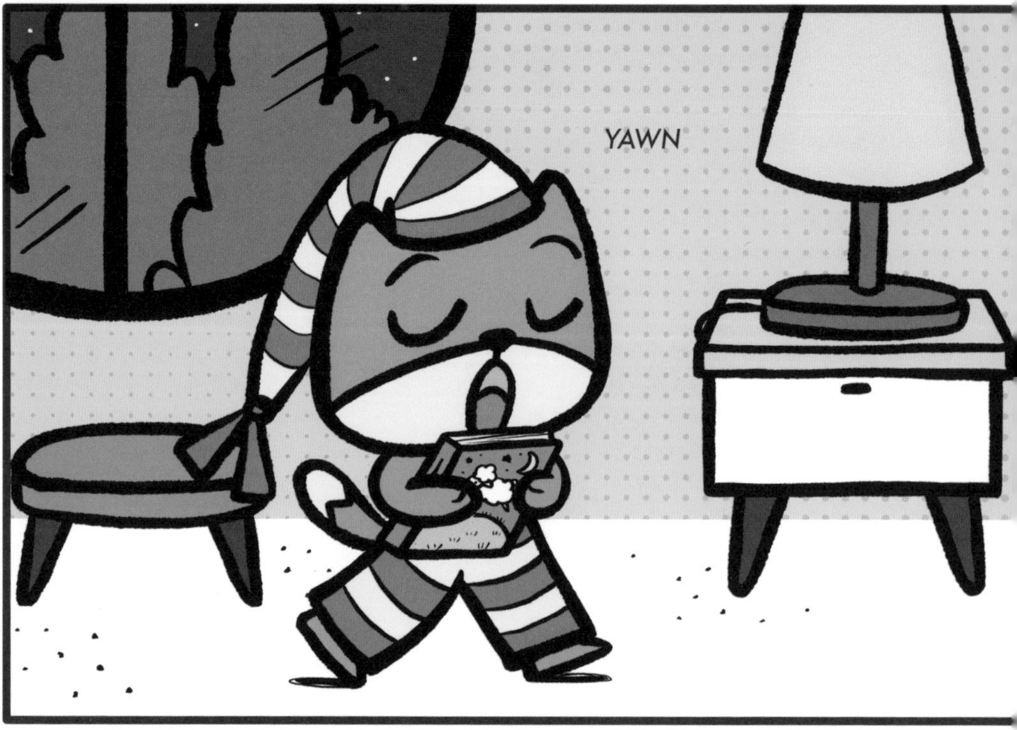
YAWN

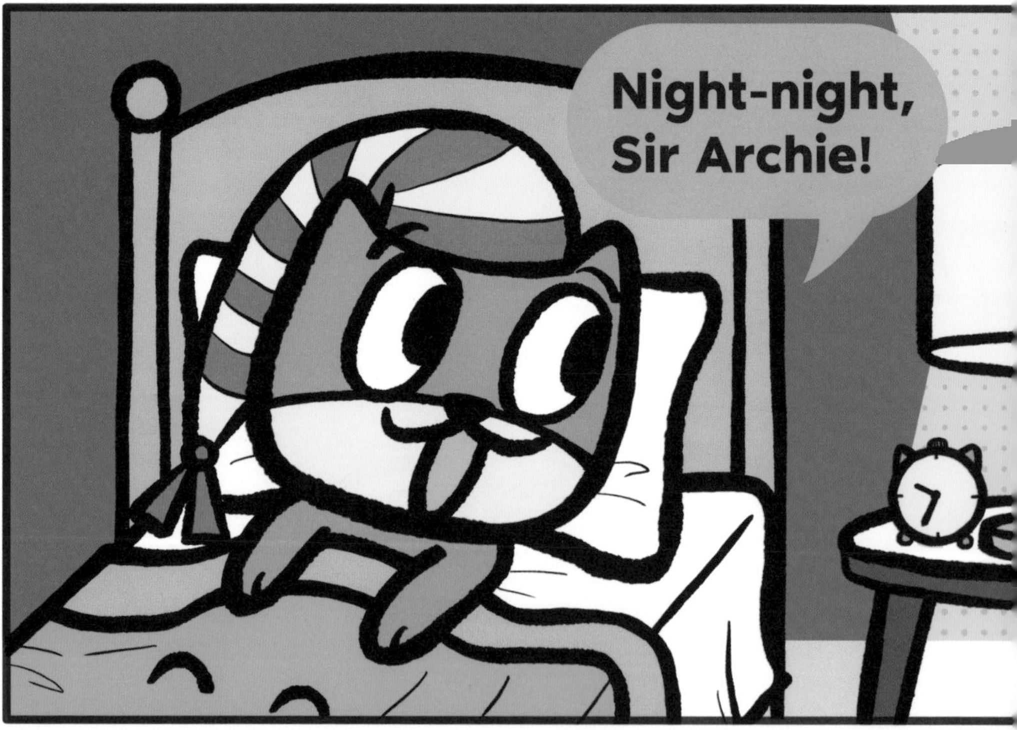
Night-night,
Sir Archie!

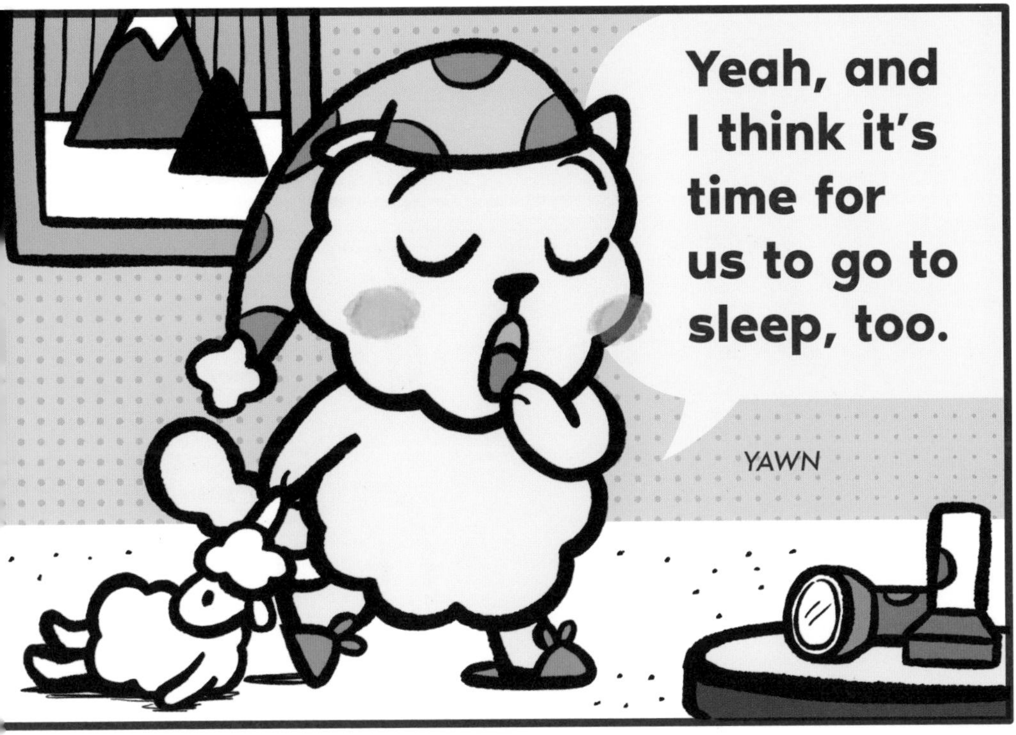
Yeah, and I think it's time for us to go to sleep, too.
YAWN

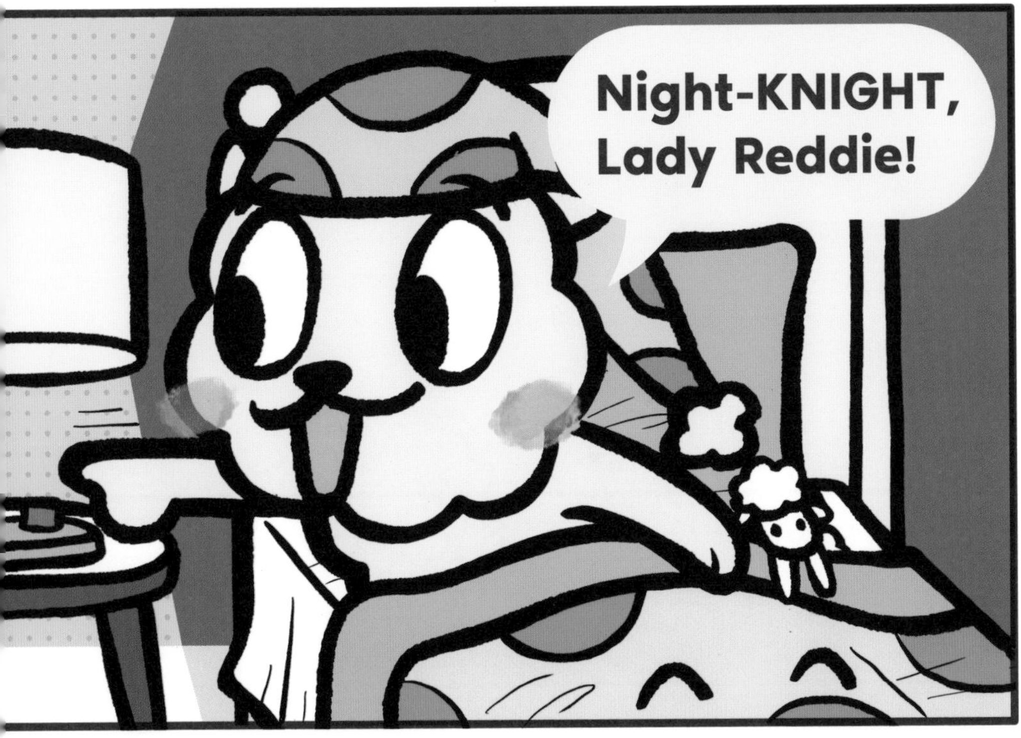
Night-KNIGHT, Lady Reddie!

MEET THE MAKERS

CANDY
draws

JAMES
writes

Candy James is a husband-and-wife creative duo originally from Hong Kong and New Zealand, but now living on a thickly forested hill in Ballarat, Australia. They are toy, graphic, and garden designers who love to make funny books for children.

What are they scared of?

Nobody laughing at their jokes.

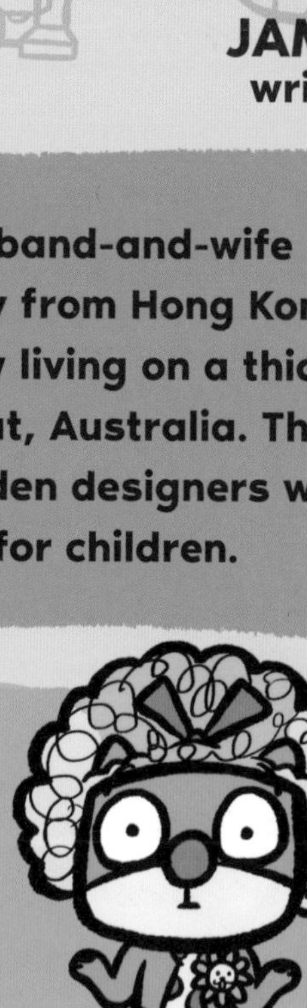